Ghostly Whispers, Secret Voices

**Seven dark and surprising tales
featuring the novella
*Ghostly Whispers***

Parker Francis

Cover Art and illustrations by Greg DiGenti
Published by Windrusher Hall Press
Ponte Vedra Beach, Florida

<u>**Praise for the Parker Francis Novels**</u>

—MATANZAS BAY—

"MATANZAS BAY is as intricate and full of surprises as an archaeological dig into old Florida's treasures and new Florida's darkest secrets."
Shamus Award-winning author Michael Wiley

"MATANZAS BAY is a Chinatown-like hall of mirrors of murder, conspiracy, and land development in St. Augustine."
Popular author of American sea fiction David Poyer

"Parker Francis has created a mystery that twists and turns like the narrow cobblestone streets and alleys of the city in which it is set."
The Florida Times-Union

—BRING DOWN THE FURIES—

"Another terrific outing for Parker Francis, who definitely delivers what readers want. He's a powerhouse storyteller and a welcome addition to the thriller genre. Hang on tight and remember to breathe."
New York Times bestselling author Steve Berry

"BRING DOWN THE FURIES is engrossing, unpredictable, and fast-paced."
Author and teacher John Dufresne

"With a finely drawn Southern setting and a crackling good plot, author Parker Francis offers up a riveting page-turner."
Deborah Sharp, author of the Mace Bauer Mysteries

—HURRICANE ISLAND—

"A rip-roaring thriller and tightly-wound mystery wrapped in one."
Paul Levine, author of bestselling mysteries and thrillers

"Parker Francis' new thriller starts with a gust and steadily increases to hurricane speeds."
Bestselling author Lisa Black

"With a murder, a double kidnapping, rising winds, and a pocketful of alligator teeth, this is the perfect storm of a mystery."
Shamus Award-winning author Michael Wiley

"*HURRICANE ISLAND* is twenty-four stormy hours and one living hell of a good time."
New York Times bestselling author Jefferson Bass

Close your eyes and listen closely to those …

GHOSTLY WHISPERS, SECRET VOICES

By Parker Francis

Seven dark and surprising tales including the novella *Ghostly Whispers*

SAVING SAM

An elderly woman and her invalid husband share their final hours together before facing eviction from their longtime home. Sometimes a house is more than a home.

TEXTING APRIL

Technology is moving rapidly, but text messages from the beyond? You'll share Nick's perplexity when a dead girl asks his help in finding her killer.

MY BROTHER, MY BURDEN

Racing to save his disturbed brother before he can harm himself, Robert gains new insights into his very special brother.

WIMMER'S LUCK

Two vicious thugs force Wimmer's wife to rob her own bank while they hold him hostage. Can the Wimmer's survive the terror-filled day?

AND PROMISES TO KEEP

A flat tire in the middle of the night on a deserted road is only the beginning of a fateful journey.

THE STRANGE CASE OF LORD BYRON'S LOVER

Writing in her journal, Mary Shelley recounts a series of perplexing events during her visit with Lord Byron—a visit that resulted in the creation of her famous Frankenstein novel, but also uncovered a remarkable mystery.

GHOSTLY WHISPERS

Desperate to find relief from the tinnitus that caused him to leave his job as a rock musician, "Mad Max" Gribbins learns the alternative can be both a blessing and a curse.

Contents

HEARING GHOSTLY WHISPERS

An Introductory Note

I've heard it said that writers live within themselves so much they start to believe those voices in their heads are real. Creating complex characters for my novels, or "Playing God," as it's sometimes called, is a mystifying experience and it's not unusual for one of my characters to talk back to me.

When a fictional character decides they want to be portrayed differently or travel a route other than the one I've outlined for them I can only shake my head and see where they take me. Of course, when the detour becomes problematic in terms of the storyline, I've been known to eliminate the troublemaker entirely.

Uncooperative characters are more common while writing long form fiction, which is why I occasionally take a break between projects and find refuge in the short story. Unlike novels, which are complex and layered structures unfolding, perhaps, over long periods of time, the short story is a drive-by glance at life. Compressed into far fewer words than a novel, the short story focuses on a literary lightning bolt striking the protagonist with some blinding insight. The Irish author Joseph O'Connor said, "A good short story is almost always about a moment of profound realization. A quiet bomb."

And sometimes the bombs are not so quiet.

In this collection you'll find stories where characters whispered to me over long periods of time, sometimes encouraging me to reach deeper into the darker recesses of my mind to find the best resolution and that moment of profound realization.

Some of these stories have been published and others have not. Some are extremely short, others more in line with the typical short story length, while one runs nearly 100 pages. Each of them will hopefully surprise you and leave you a bit uneasy about the human condition. A series of title page illustrations by the noted graphic artist Greg DiGenti has been added to enhance your reading enjoyment. And if you'll forgive my further interruptions, I've provided brief introductions to each of the stories to give you insights into the gestation process that began with my own ghostly whispers.

As a boy, I loved the stories of O'Henry, so it's not surprising that most of these tales will have a twist at the end. They may shock you and perhaps you'll question the mental state of an author who admits to hearing strange voices in his head.

Let me assure you I have them under control. I really do. But the question is will you be able to say the same after reading these seven tales? I seriously doubt you're in any danger of hearing ghostly whispers or secret voices. At least I don't think you will.

Enjoy!

Parker Francis

The First Whisper

Story ideas can blossom on the most barren of terrains. Sometimes hearing a friend's experience might trigger a "what if" question that turns an anecdote into a story premise. Other times we might read an item in the paper or see it on the news and where most normal people will offer a *tsk tsk* and go on about their business, the writer hears the very same account and it settles into that mutant part of their brain where plot ideas are born. I've heard of writers who awakened from a dream so vivid they swear the story had been written out in advance by their sleeping minds. And maybe it had.

Saving Sam came to life from two very different sources—one of them the countless news stories we endured during the economic downturn of the last decade. Tens of thousands of homeowners were forced into foreclosure by their banks. Many faced eviction from houses they'd lived in for years. I wondered how this might affect someone who was about to be evicted from the home where they'd shared intimate moments with their spouse; had raised children, struggled and loved together.

The other source was an image so strong I couldn't get it out of my head. The image was that of an elderly woman pushing a wheelchair down a long, dark hallway. I'm not sure where it came from, but it became the opening to *Saving Sam*. I tried to put myself in the place of these two characters—to walk (and be pushed) through this old house flooded with so many memories. How would they feel knowing that with the morning's light would come a banker and a sheriff's deputy to enforce a judge's order of eviction? Would they be bitter or resigned to their fate?

Ah, but life is cruel, isn't it? The whispers I heard kept telling me that although life throws us some curve balls now and then, humans are resourceful and surprising creatures. At least the creatures residing in a writer's head. But let's not linger in the past any longer since you have a date with Annie and Sam.

saving
sam

SAVING SAM

Dark and dank, the long hallway cleaved a path through their downstairs rooms. Pushing Sam's wheelchair down the dim corridor, Annie took note of the darkened overhead light bulb. It had burned out last week. Let the bank take care of it, she thought.

Carpeting had once covered the bare floors of the hallway, but Sheila, the feral cat she'd rescued, had turned it into her personal litter box. Nothing Annie tried would remove the sharp, acrid stink and she eventually pulled up the carpet and padding. Even after all these years, she still detected the faint odor of cat urine hanging in the air. Or maybe she only imagined it since Sam never complained.

She continued pushing Sam toward the study, taking note of every crack in the wall, the warped baseboard. Annie knew this house as well as the favorite sweater she wore nearly everyday during the winter months. Like the house, the sweater was threadbare, but she would never throw it out. It was the first thing Sam had ever given her. She loved that old sweater and would never part with it.

She couldn't say the same about the house. They'd be going their separate ways soon enough. Which was why she was making this one last tour, pushing Sam along the narrow hallway, listening to the clicking of the misaligned wheel on the ancient wheelchair, the creaking of old wood planks.

"You're awfully quiet, Annie-bug."

"I was just thinking we should have had the house painted. It looks like no one's lived here for years. What are they going to think of us?"

"Why do you care?"

She glanced down at Sam's bald head, the shiny jaundiced scalp daubed with red splotches and dotted with a few yellowish hairs.

"I said why do you care what they think. It's not like we're selling the house or expecting company for dinner. They're taking our house. Am I right?"

She remained quiet. Sam was right, but that didn't make it any easier. She kept pushing the wheelchair. At the study she paused and looked inside to make sure the movers hadn't missed anything. Only the area rug remained. Frayed at the edges with holes worn through in several places, it should have been thrown out years ago. But now it lay there, forgotten and unwanted. Exactly how Annie felt.

How long had it been since she'd been anywhere, seen anything but the inside of these walls? She knew there was a world out there. She heard cars passing. Occasional shouts and the sounds of laughter from the O'Brien twins next door. On the other side, Mrs. Grasso's TV was blaring so loudly she could hear Alex Trebek giving the answers.

Her house was one of a dozen nearly identical row houses on Newbury Street, packed brick against brick like a shelf of books. Annie knew she hadn't done a good job of taking care of the house. The plumbing was a mess, and it badly needed a coat of paint. But what did that matter now? Tomorrow morning it would be someone else's problem.

"Are you going to walk all night?" Sam asked, his voice breaking through her self-pity.

"No, I just want to be sure we don't leave anything important behind."

"Speak up, will you. And can you stop for a minute? I'm tired of talking to the empty walls. Come around here where I can see you."

His voice had a pleading quality, and guilt seeped into her gut like the drip, drip, drip of acid. She had tried so hard to save Sam from all of this. She could handle the indignities of foreclosure, but Sam relied on her for everything. She knew he would have a hard time adapting to their new home—if a one-bedroom rental trailer could be called a home.

She braked the old wheelchair and stepped around so he could see her. "I'm sorry, Sam. This whole foreclosure thing has made me so angry, I feel like I'm going to explode."

Only Sam's eyes turned upward to meet her own eyes. His face, once broad and handsome, always smiling with sparkling eyes, had lost most of its form, falling in on itself leaving sharp angles of bone and ribbons of cartilage.

"It might look like we've entered the storm clouds, but there's always sunshine ahead. Just think about the day we moved into this house, and—"

"That was our first mistake. I told you nothing good would come from us buying a house we couldn't afford."

"Nothing good? Baby, have you forgotten the good times we had in this house?"

Was he serious? "Good times!" She spit the words out like grapeshot from a cannon. "We're in foreclosure, for God's sake, and you talk about good times. The bank is coming to take our house in the morning. Can't you get that through your thick Irish skull?"

She regretted the words the moment they escaped her mouth. But she knew he wouldn't care.

"Sure they are, but what does it matter? Think of the memories. We've had the time of our lives in this house and they can't take that away from us."

She studied him wondering if he was playing with her. But no, that was Sam. The eternal optimist. Still the same after everything that's happened to them. Which is exactly why she fell in love and married the man. Oh, she got plenty of grief from her family, her father in particular. *"Angelina, please don't do this,"* he had begged her. *"He's an Irishman. He'll stay drunk all the time, and in the end leave you alone with your bambinos."*

Her father was an old-fashioned man with narrow views of the world. In the end, he was the one who left her. Less than a year after they were married, her father collapsed and died from a massive heart attack. She hadn't had a lot of luck with the men in her life, which was why she wanted to save Sam from what was about to happen.

She held onto the arm of the wheelchair and squatted in front of Sam. Instantly, her arthritis took issue with the new position, sending a bolt of pain down her spine. Annie ignored the aches, and looked at Sam, taking in the shrunken limbs, frozen and gnarled like some long-buried fossil. He'd been a quadriplegic for nearly twenty-eight years, unable to move anything but his mouth.

Despite herself she smiled. That mouth of his. Always in motion. He was a talker from the moment they met, and she loved him all the more for it. Sam never ran out of things to talk about. The night he proposed, he promised her they'd be rich. They were sitting in a booth at the Emerald Rose, him working his way through his second Guinness, her nursing a wine cooler, Sam declaring his love, and telling her how they'd travel the world, see the pyramids, the Nile. But first he'd take her to *the land of his fathers,* Cork, and Killarney.

Sam had been so convincing. She was captivated by his passion, over-whelmed by his enthusiasm for life. They never made it to Ireland, but he did take her to Niagara Falls for their honeymoon. Maybe if the accident hadn't happened. But she didn't believe that either. Just like she didn't believe they had the time of their lives in this house. Her smile disappeared and a hot flame of resentment ignited inside her.

"Damn it, Sam, memories don't mean a thing at this point except to drive you crazy. Do you think I can pay the mortgage with memories? Will Mr. Kresser tell me the bank changed its mind even though I haven't paid them a cent in eight months because we have so many memories tucked away in this house?"

She tasted bitter bile in her mouth and caught herself looking at Sam as though he were an imbecile child.

Annie patted him on the knee and pushed herself up, feeling *Mr. Arthritis* come a-calling once again. She laid a hand on Sam's skeletal shoulder, wonder-ing how she had done it for all these years. Tending to him like he was a baby, unable to do anything for himself. Enduring the hardship of being a caregiver, working to keep their spirits up, and not always succeeding. But she had done her best to save Sam.

She moved behind the wheelchair again and pushed him down the hall toward the empty bedroom, thinking that he might stop talking if she kept moving. Fat chance, she thought.

"Come on, Annie," his gravelly voice cut through her bitter thoughts as though he could read her mind. "Okay, we've fallen on some rough patches lately, but we'll bounce back. We'll come through—"

She pushed him into the bedroom before answering. "Do you ever listen to yourself, Sam?" She cut her eyes to his shiny scalp for a moment and away toward the bare wall where she pictured the colorful circus wallpaper that had brightened the room before she painted over it.

"Bounce back? Bounce back from thirty-five years of misery? Like I said, no good ever came from this house."

"There you go again. Look around you. This was Todd's room. Can you see his bed there against the wall? The elephants and the ringmaster behind the bed? Open your eyes and look, Annie. I can see it all."

"I don't see anything," she said. But she did. The images appeared to her as fresh and bright as the day they glued the circus mural to the wall.

"Do you remember the bookshelf we put up there to hold his baseball trophy and his model airplanes? And all his drawings? He taped them over the wallpaper, said he was too old for circus stuff. But didn't you love those drawings? Rocket ships, Popeye fighting the huge ape."

Annie found herself caught up in his excitement despite herself. "Yeah, he called it Popeye and King Korn."

"King Korn. That's right, King Korn." Sam laughed and she felt herself smiling along with him. She hadn't thought of those drawings in forever. What an imagination her Todd had.

"And you said nothing good happened here. Think about his birthday parties. Remember the time I dressed up as a clown and—"

"And you tripped over those huge shoes and nearly fell into the birthday cake." Now she was laughing out loud.

"Yes, yes. Toddy and his friends thought I was the funniest clown ever."

She turned to Sam, seeing the painted clown face for a moment before it faded away. In its place she saw Sam's watery blue eyes, the breathing tubes emerging from his nostrils, and waxy skin shining unnaturally as though it was created of silicon and plastic in a chemist's lab. She laid a hand on his cheek, felt the sharp outline of his cheekbone against her hand.

"You were a very funny clown, Sam. I'll give you that." She pivoted away from the wall of memories, and wheeled him back into the hall.

"On the move again. My Annie can't sit still tonight?"

"Can you blame me? In another twelve hours, I have to turn this house over to the bank."

"You did your best, baby."

"It wasn't enough."

"But you were a tiger, don't you know?"

She was in the kitchen now, stopping in front of the sink with its long counter where she'd made cakes for Todd's birthday parties, fixed their meals.

"I gave them fits, didn't I?"

Sam laughed again. This time, the laugh emerged louder and longer, coming from a place she couldn't imagine. She hadn't heard him laugh like that in years. Annie couldn't help herself and felt the laughter erupting from deep in her chest and bubble out in the form of a rolling chortle that shook her large frame.

"Those bankers didn't know what hit them when they tangled with you."

"Got that right. I told them they'd have to carry me out of this house."

He laughed again, and it made her heart quicken to see him enjoying himself. It almost looked like the years were falling away from him.

"That's right. You gave them everything they could handle and more."

She shook her head, remembering the shouting matches with Mr. Kresser. Poor man. He was only doing his job, but this was her house they were trying to take away. Their last conversation came back to her as she rolled the memories over in her mind.

"I'm terribly sorry, Mrs. McFall. You've been in default for eight months."

Kresser looked down at the files on his desk as though the answer was somewhere in those sheets of paper. Annie hated the way the bank had transformed her life—her past, present and future—into a series of numbers. Kresser was a lanky man with thinning brown hair and a prominent nose. He looked up, directing his gaze to a spot several inches below her eyes.

"We've given you every opportunity to make it right, Mrs. McFall. Our—"

"So you're going to snatch an old woman's home? Here I am living on Social Security. The only thing I have is the house I've lived in for thirty-five years, and you're taking it away. What kind of country is this?"

"Our hands are tied, Mrs. McFall. I've told you that. Maybe if the economy wasn't so bad, and the whole housing market in such a mess, we'd have a bit more latitude." His hands flopped upwards like he'd lost control of them.

He looked so miserable Annie almost felt sorry for him. "So I get punished because your bank was too greedy to use the common sense God gave a pumpkin. You know I've paid more interest on that house, probably twice what it's worth."

"Yes ma'am, but you took out the second mortgage back in…" he paused, his hands moving quickly to the file, fingering the pages, obviously eager for something to do.

"You don't have to give me my history. You know damn well why I took out that second mortgage. My husband's accident. The bills. The insurance money was gone. What choice did I have?"

"Annie, are you all right?"

Sam's voice transported her from the banker's office back to the kitchen where he sat patiently waiting for her.

"Yeah, I'm fine. Just peachy keen."

She hated that her bitterness spilled over onto Sam. None of it was his fault. The truck that plowed into him, pancaking the car, making an invalid of him, taking … Funny how your life can change in the blink of an eye. Happily married with the perfect family one moment, the next …

Her eyes welled and she fought back tears, forcing herself to look down at Sam. She stood behind him, hands gripping the wheelchair handles, thinking she needed to remain strong for him. She couldn't save their home, but she could still save Sam.

"What are you doing back there? Sounds like you're crying. You're not crying, are you Annie?"

"Just rinsing my eyes, baby. That's all."

"You know big girls don't cry."

How many times had he told her that? It used to make her laugh when they were first married. Later she'd smile and agree with him, although she knew it was far from the truth. Big girls cried all the time, but he still used the ridiculous phrase each time she felt the blues sneak up on her and needed a good cry to work it out of her system. She no longer thought it was funny.

"You're wrong, Sam," she snapped before she could catch herself. "Big girls do cry, and I wish you'd stop spouting your moronic clichés."

"Now, Annie, anger never solved a thing. You have so much to be thankful for. Come here where I can see your beautiful face."

Thankful! Red lights flashed across her vision. She felt waves of heat rise up her neck, over her face. Instead of walking around in front of the chair, Annie yanked one of the handles of the chair and spun it around with all her strength. She was a big woman with arms made strong from muscling Sam in and out of bed, in and out of the chair, each and every day.

Sam shifted violently against the strap holding him erect in the wheelchair, his head flopping like a rag doll's. The oxygen tube flew from his nostrils. His body shifted in the chair, and Annie watched in horror as he slid through the restraining strap toward the floor.

She rushed to him, her hands flying to catch him. "Oh, I'm so sorry, Sam. Are you all right?" She bent over him, placing her hands under his arms and carefully lifting him so he sat straight in the chair once again. She brushed gently at the frayed flannel robe covering his bony chest as though brushing crumbs away. She replaced the oxygen tube in his nose and gave him a weak smile.

"I'm sorry, baby. You're not hurt, are you." Her eyes pleaded with him to talk to her.

"That's the most fun I've had in years," he said, his voice more ragged than usual.

"Oh, Sam, what am I going to do with you?"

Annie slumped against the refrigerator, felt the compressor kick in, pulsing against her back. She smiled at Sam, who looked at her expectantly, as he did everyday. Like a dog wagging its tail watching food poured into its bowl. No, that wasn't fair. She reminded herself that none of this was his fault, but that didn't make it any easier. The days of drudgery, the uncertainty, calls from bill collectors.

She'd always been a strong woman, and God knows she was always there for Sam. But sometimes she wished for a man to take care of her for once. A man with strong legs and arms who could hold her and make her forget her life of pain. Sam had tried to tell her to move on with her life. Shortly after the accident, he told her, "Leave me, Annie. You're still young. Go out and find yourself a real man."

Stubborn as ever, she refused to listen. "Sam, there's no way I'd leave you, so shut up and get over yourself."

Sure, she had every reason to feel sorry for herself. To break down and curse the world for leaving her in these circumstances. But she wasn't going to leave him alone. Not after what they'd been through together.

"Is there any food in that thing?"

"You mean the refrigerator?"

"Uh-huh."

"Are you hungry?"

"No, I thought maybe you could make omelets in the morning. One last time before they come."

Sam and his omelets. He could eat them every day. She did make a mean omelet, though. "I think we still have some eggs left. So sure. Once more for old times sake."

"That's my Annie." He looked at her, his eyes shining through the misty cast. "I'm getting tired. Maybe you should put me to bed. Get ready for the big day."

Annie understood. She lived with exhaustion. It existed deep in her very core, saturated her bones. "Yes, I'm pretty beat myself," she said to her Sam. "Why don't we get some sleep."

She wheeled him toward the room with the electric bed and the medical air mattress to prevent bed sores. As she hefted him onto the bed and settled him on his back, careful not to crimp his breathing tube, he kept his eyes on her. The sparkle was back in the blue eyes, and for a moment, she saw the man she had walked down the aisle with. She remembered them together in a very different kind of bed, doing things that she hadn't let herself think about in years. Unbidden, a flush of heat swept over her.

The memories were so strong she almost shivered with delight, feeling his weight on her, his murmurings of love in her ear. Annie gazed at Sam, and maybe it was a trick of the dim light, but his hair seemed fuller, darker. His smile brighter.

"Goodnight, hon." She patted his frail arm before turning to leave.

"Annie."

She turned back to him. "What is it?"

"Remember we always said we'd never go to bed mad at each other."

"I'm not mad at you."

"I know, but this mess with the bank has you knotted up, and I hate to see you like this."

"Well, I haven't much of a choice in the matter, do I?"

He studied her face for a moment before speaking and she felt his eyes taking in every line on her wrinkled face. Surely, there was not much of the old Annie there for him to love.

"This is our last night together in this house. Would you sleep with me to-night?"

Her eyes widened as she looked down on Sam in his hospital bed, totally immobile, tubes extending from his nose, the oxygen tank rumbling in the background. "Oh, baby, I don't know if that's such a good idea."

"Come on, Annie. One last time. Just like we used to before…"

Annie stared at him, her heart warming under his gaze. "Of course I will. Just like we used to."

She moved to the other side of the bed and carefully settled in beside him, easing her large frame over until she felt his body against hers. Annie's left arm gently settled over his inert form, her hand slipping beneath his back to hold him in an awkward embrace. She felt his ribs, his twisted spine with the brace supporting him. Annie put her face against his and felt the warmth of tears against her cheek.

She was so tired, she knew she'd be asleep as soon as she closed her eyes. Instead, she imagined his arms wrapping around her body, his hands kneading her back, his mouth moving from her neck to her breast. She shook off the vision, kissed him softly on the forehead.

"Goodnight, Sam. I'll see you in the morning."

Walter Kresser stood in the door of the bedroom, a sheriff's deputy who looked like he might have graduated from high school the year before, stood beside him.

"Guess that's why she didn't answer the door," the deputy said.

Kresser didn't say anything, his eyes were glued to the lone figure curled up on the old hospital bed. She lay on her side, one arm extended as though draped over someone else. But there was no one else. A vintage wheelchair sat next to the bed, one wheel slightly bent, the leather backing cracked. He thought about the last time he'd seen Mrs. McFall and a shiver rippled along his spine. "It's probably for the best," he mumbled.

What's that?"

Kresser forced himself to turn from the bedroom scene and faced the deputy. "This poor woman has gone though so much in her life. You don't know how I was dreading facing her this morning."

"Well, that's what happens when people don't pay their bills. They got no one to blame but themselves."

Kresser looked at the deputy, thinking he was so young to be so wrong. "You think so? Let me tell you about Annie McFall. Twenty-eight years ago, her husband Sam, who had been a young sheriff's deputy just like you, was driving back from Shutter Park. He was one of the coaches on his son Todd's little league team. Todd was in the front seat, and I'm sure they were caught up in the excitement of the afternoon, a father and son outing together. Do you have any kids, Deputy…" he looked at the name plate on the young officer's uniform. "Deputy Denton?"

"No sir, I'm not even married yet."

"Well, I'm sure one day you will, and maybe you'll understand what I'm saying. They were stopped at the light at Willard Avenue and Brockton—"

"That's a bad intersection."

"The light changed. Sam started across the intersection when a truck roared through, plowing into their car on the passenger side. The driver had been drinking, thought he could beat the light. Must have been going fifty miles an hour when he hit them. Flipped the car over. The boy was killed instantly, Sam turned into a vegetable. Left him totally paralyzed."

"My God." Deputy Denton's eyes went wide and he turned towards the woman lying on the bed. "So what happened?"

"After months of hospitalization and rehab, all their savings and insurance money were gone. Annie brought Sam home. The doctors tried to tell her there was no way she could care for him by herself. That Sam wasn't going to live much longer, anyway."

He glanced at the body before shifting back to the deputy. He shook his head and gave him a slight smile. "If you knew Annie McFall you'd know you couldn't tell her a thing. Sam was the only family she had left, and she wasn't going to leave him behind. I can't imagine how she did it, but somehow, she kept him alive for almost eight years."

"And what happened after that?"

"She lived here alone, never remarried, never asking for help. I'm thinking she didn't have the best education, but she got work at what she could, cleaning other people's houses, doing their wash and cooking just to make ends meet. She took a second mortgage on the house to get over some of their medical bills, and she was real good about making her payments, until…"

"Until this year?"

"Uh-huh. We carried her as long as we could, but with thirty percent of our loans in default, the bank had no choice but to foreclose."

Deputy Denton eyed Kresser suspiciously. "I guess not." He scratched his head with the legal document in his hand. "I better call for an ambulance and the medical examiner."

Kresser nodded in agreement, taking one last look at Annie McFall. "Funny thing, though."

"What's that?"

"She told me we'd have to carry her out of this house. She was spot on with that prediction."

Kresser turned his back on the old woman, but felt her presence follow him as he walked along the darkened hallway.

THE SECOND WHISPER

You've probably heard comments from old-timers (and I include myself in that category) lamenting the changes technology has made on our society.

"People don't talk to one another anymore," they say. "And the kids, always with a phone in their hands."

Some wags have even suggested future generations will be born with over-sized thumbs as evolution adapts to our nonstop texting. It makes you wonder how the lyrics might change if Paul Lynde were around today to sing, "What's the Matter With Kids Today?"

Surely, today's kids are smarter as a result of their early introduction to the Internet and computer games. Most ten year olds are more technologically adept than those of us who lived at least half of our lives prior to Steve Jobs' contributions to changing the way we communicate.

Texting April grew out of this growing phenomenon I observed as well as the desire to dip a toe into the same waters Stephen King had been swimming in for so many years. As it turned out, *Texting April* was less Stephen King and more Alfred Hitchcock. In the story, technology is pushed past the limits of natural law into the supernatural world when our hero, Nick, receives a text message from someone who is no longer among the living.

Turn your phone off for a few minutes and wade into the dark waters with me. But you might want to keep your thumbs limbered. Who knows when you might receive a text from the great beyond?

texting
april
2:58
April

TEXTING APRIL

Nick stared at the lifeless squirrel and thought of April. Hands on hips, breathing hard from his run, he nudged the squirrel with the toe of his running shoe. He didn't expect it to move.

It didn't.

Slivers of sunlight filtered through the branches of the oak, casting spectral shadows, shifting shape with each gust of wind. Nick imagined the path of the squirrel's fall. The baby squirrel may have been testing the outside world for the first time. Finding instead the cold reality of death before it had time to truly live. Just like April, dead before her eleventh birthday.

This was the first day his parents had allowed him to run in the neighborhood since April's death. Not that he blamed them. The murder of the ten-year-old girl had stunned them all, coming only six months after the killing of another young girl. Waves of suspicion rolled over every family in their little community. Paranoia ruled. Children weren't allowed to play outdoors. For sale signs sprung up like mushrooming fairy rings after a heavy rain.

For a brief time the nation's attention shifted from war zones to focus on the tragic deaths. Reporters from the national news services jostled one another to claim front row positions for the tear-filled news conference held by April's parents. They knocked on neighbors' doors, stopped people in the streets, asking questions, sticking microphones in their faces.

It didn't last long. Another disaster in another corner of the country, and the CNN and Fox News vans moved on. The police continued to search for clues, although after three months there had been few, if any, leads. Parents through-out the neighborhood hovered over their children, walking them to school bus stops, sequestering them inside their homes after school. He'd never seen the streets so deserted.

Nick ran cross-country for his school, and practiced on the track surrounding the high school football field. But that wasn't the same as running through the woods, and he had pleaded with his parents for weeks before they finally relented. He told them the killer had probably split for California or some foreign country by now. He wasn't sure they bought that argument, but saw the logic when he said, "Anyway, I'm a fifteen-year-old boy, not a ten-year-old girl. I'm not his type."

They finally agreed, but insisted he bring his iPhone with him. He would have anyway since he liked to listen to music as he ran. These woods were perfect for his training. A path had been beaten through the woods by hundreds of kids taking a shortcut to the elementary school several blocks away. He remembered when he was one of those kids trooping along the path with his friends, backpacks stuffed with books and lunch bags, moving slowly in the morning, running and jostling one another on the way home in the afternoon.

Nick looked at the squirrel once again, noticing for the first time ants crawling over the animal's face, across its open, staring eyes. He knew in a few days nature would work its disappearing act, reducing the infant squirrel to a scattering of fur and bones. He understood this was all part of the natural cycle of life and death. Ashes to ashes; dust to dust.

Again, his thoughts turned to the dead girl. He didn't actually know April, but both of their mothers were in a garden club together. He'd seen April playing in her yard from time to time. Cute little kid. Curly blond hair. Friendly, too. She always smiled and waved when he ran by on his way to the woods. He felt a knot in his stomach when he thought about her.

Nick turned away from the squirrel, adjusted his ear buds, tapped the music icon on his iPhone, and loped away. He filled his lungs with the warm spring air, knowing it wouldn't be long before the heat, humidity and bugs made these afternoon runs uncomfortable. Now, though, dark clouds were dueling with the afternoon sun, turning what had been a brilliant blue sky into a gloomy cloak. Rain was in the forecast, and it looked like he'd have to hurry if he didn't want to get wet.

He followed the path around a sharp curve and accelerated through the final stretch leading back to the street. Just as Nick was reaching his top speed, he felt the vibration in his pocket and heard the electronic chime of an incoming text message. He was certain it was his mother, the worrywart, checking on him. Without breaking stride, Nick pulled the device from his pocket and looked at the screen. The text message jumped out at him.

Nick blinked once, twice, his heart leaping into another gear. A rush of heat rose from his chest, sluicing through his head until he felt like he was about to faint. Some internal governor pulled a switch in his brain and his legs stopped their motion. He pulled up abruptly, legs melting beneath him, and plopped down in the middle of the dirt path, a little cloud of dust spreading out from around his butt. He was clutching the iPhone so tightly his hand started to cramp.

He closed his eyes thinking he must have misread the message. When he looked again he saw he hadn't imagined it. Unbelieving, he read it again.

nick she knows who killed me. april

What kind of pervert would send him a message like that? He flipped through his mental contact list, trying to decide which of his friends or acquaintances would pull such a slimeball trick. He couldn't think of any.

He studied the words until the screen turned itself off, the message disappearing as though it had never been there. He thumbed the on button again hoping it would be gone, that maybe he was having some kind of runner's hallucination. But the message was still there. His hand shook with rage, but he fingered the reply button and thumbed rapidly, the anger building with each letter he pressed.

i cant blieve how wacked out u r who is this?

Nick tapped the Send button. As much as he hoped that was the end of it, he had a feeling it was far from over.

"Amazing," he said aloud. He shook his head in disbelief and repeated, "Amazing."

A mockingbird responded with a harsh *Chewk!* repeated three times, and he scanned the tree line searching for the bird. Instead he saw a huge silken web between two scrub myrtle branches just inches away from his face. Hanging upside down in the center of the web was a large black and yellow spider that seemed to be staring at him with malevolent eyes.

The spider unnerved him nearly as much as the text message, and he jumped to his feet. Nick decided it was time to finish his run and get back home. Before he took a single step, the iPhone vibrated and the tone alerted him to another message.

Despite the uneasy feeling in the pit of his stomach, he read the text bubble below his reply:

U need to ask her who killed me

Nick almost threw the phone to the ground. He wanted to stomp on it, grind it into shards of glass and mashed computer chips. Instead he took a deep breath and let it out slowly through his nostrils. He did it one more time before touching the screen to life.

He thumbed his response.

who r u? april's dead and u know it

Tapping the Send button, Nick realized he was playing right into this guy's game. As long as he kept rising to the bait, the asshole would keep playing him—like a fish fighting and jumping to dislodge the hook, being pulled ever closer to the fisherman. But the furies in his head gave him no other choice.

Within moments, the phone chimed again.

it's me april. hard 2 believe i know

Not hard to believe. Freaking impossible to believe. There was no doubt April was dead. He'd seen them carry her body from the house. He and his family went to her funeral service. His parents had spoken to the police and learned they thought a serial killer was behind the girls' murders. April's mother had even confided to his mother that whoever killed her daughter had taken the girl's charm bracelet. Nick knew from watching *Criminal Minds* on TV that serial killers liked to take trophies to remind them of their victims.

He decided not to give this nut job the attention he was obviously seeking. He powered off the phone and put it in his pocket. Nick ran for home, rounding a sharp curve in the path where a heavy canopy of oak branches cast deep shadows over the patch of woods. Goose bumps shuttled across his shoulders.

The phone came to life, chiming and vibrating in the pocket of his running shorts. He ignored it and ran on. He was through acting like a hooked fish. Ahead of him he saw the end of the path and the little park that marked the beginning of his residential neighborhood. Ten more minutes and he'd be home. The phone chimed three more times in rapid succession. He fought the compulsion to pull it out of his pocket and read *her* message.

No! It's not her, he mentally chastised himself. April is dead. This isn't a *Ghost Whisperer* episode. This is real life. Nick tried to stoke the outrage he'd felt when he saw the first text, pile on the hatred and bile that had overwhelmed him. He dug deep inside, found a few wisps of anger, and channeled it into his run, digging deep, setting a swifter pace.

Overhead, the dark clouds had prevailed, banishing the sun. He felt the wind pick up. Splashes of rain gashed at his face. Within minutes he was plowing through puddles, kicking up muddy spatters on his legs and arms. The phone vibrated against his thigh pulling at him with such intensity he stopped running, chest heaving.

Nick watched in amazement as his right hand moved steadily toward his pocket as though it belonged to someone else. His mind told him there was nothing to be gained by this gruesome game of give and take. But his hand was no longer controlled by the nerve impulses swooping down from his brain. He attempted to pull his hand away, regain control over his body, but his fingers snaked into the pocket and he felt them clamp around the phone. His thumb brought the screen to life and his hand carried it up to his face as though this had been his plan all along.

A babble of voices screamed at him not to look, to close his eyes, to toss his $300 device into the bushes and run away. Nick suppressed the voices and read the text message.

I'm really april. Kelly knows who killed me. Make her tell u

Nick had been convinced the text messages were nothing more than a cruel hoax, but icy fingers of doubt were now creeping along his spine. He'd read stories, seen movies and TV shows about restless spirits, ghosts contacting their loved ones. Fiction is just a reflection of reality, isn't it? And didn't his Sunday school teachers always preach about life after death?

The hand holding the phone tingled as though the device was emitting a low voltage electric current. It was prodding him to respond. Without consciously knowing what he was doing, his thumbs began moving across the board, tapping the letters more rapidly than he would have thought possible.

ok april, tell me who Kelly is

The phone chimed and there was her reply in the bubble.

she was my best friend. kelly lives behind us on cottage ln - green house

Nick felt his heart thumping in his chest. Christ, what if she was telling the truth? He realized he had switched pronouns and was thinking of the mystery texter as a *she*. But how could the dead reach out and send him a text message? It was too much for him to get his mind around and as he struggled to make sense of it, the iPhone chimed again.

**r u still there? did u see my last message?
kelly knows who killed me. U need to find out**

He thumbed a quick reply…

Then what? Tell the police?

and tapped Send.
Now the messages were appearing almost instantaneously.

if that's what you want, but police will think ur crazy

He knew she was right. Getting text messages from the grave. Sure, and we have a straight jacket just your size.
He wrote back:

Ok. I'll see what she knows

Nick grew up attending church like most of his friends. He was taught that God loved him and looked after good people. Nick questioned if God was watching when his dog disappeared and they later found him stuffed in a neighbor's garbage can, his neck broken. He was ten at the time, and realized that unlike what happened on TV shows, people often went unpunished for their crimes. The next year, a boy he knew drowned in the neighborhood pool one night, and the slender filaments of belief snapped completely.
Maybe he was wrong. If April could contact him from the great beyond,

there must be an afterlife. And if Kelly knew who killed April, shouldn't he do something about it?

Nick went directly to the green house on Cottage Lane. When he saw the house, he decided he had probably seen Kelly. He'd run all over this neighborhood since he'd joined the cross country team. He'd seen kids playing in the street and in their yards. Now that he thought about it, he'd probably seen April and Kelly playing together right here in this yard. But now the yard was empty. The entire street was deserted. Any kids brave enough to play outside had been chased indoors by the thunderstorm.

There were no cars in the driveway, and Nick figured Kelly, like many of her contemporaries, was probably a latch key kid. He guessed she was inside studying or watching television. The home, a split-level ranch style like many others in the neighborhood, backed up to a section of the woods and was relatively isolated.

Nick went around to the back door and listened. He heard the sound of the TV and tried the doorknob. It was locked. He knocked and called out, "Kelly."

The volume on the television set dipped—sounded like a *Hannah Montana* episode. He heard soft footsteps padding toward the back door.

"Who is it?" She didn't sound frightened, only curious.

"I'm Nick. I live a couple of streets away, and April …" *How could he put this without sounding insane?* "I knew April and she gave me something that I thought you might like to have."

Kelly was quiet for a long time. Nick heard the wail of a siren coming from the highway running behind their neighborhood. It faded into the distance and he wondered if someone was being rushed to the hospital. He stared at the door, listening for any sign that Kelly was still there. He imagined he could hear her breathing behind the door, and doubted she'd open the door to a stranger. He was about to give up when he heard the lock click and the door swung open.

It turned out that Kelly didn't know who killed April. Nick ran home and jumped in the shower to wash the sweat and mud from his body. He tried to make sense of the text messages. What did they mean? Why did he get them? And if they were from April, why did she tell him Kelly knew her killer when it was obvious Kelly didn't have a clue?

By the time he finished showering, dressed, and did his homework, it was almost time for his father to come home. His mother had already alerted him to the fact dinner was nearly ready. He went out to the living room and found his mother on the phone.

"Good God, no. Not again." She held a quivering hand up to her face and stared at Nick, eyes filled with horror.

"What is it?" he mouthed.

She waved him off with a fluttering hand.

Outside, he heard the sounds of sirens again. This time they were moving closer, growing louder.

His mother hung up the phone and nearly stumbled as she stepped toward him. Nick grabbed her, and she wrapped her arms around him.

"What's wrong?" he asked, feeling her tremble against him.

"There's … there's been another one." She was sobbing now. "They found another little girl. Dead. Just like April." She pushed away from him and staggered to a dining room chair. "This can't be happening." She raised her hands to her face and sobbed.

Nick wasn't sure what to do, how to feel. He hated seeing his mother like this. He put an arm around her, squeezing her shoulder momentarily. "This is terrible," he said. "Maybe we should move from here."

His mother dropped her hands and looked at him. She started to say something, but only nodded.

"Dad will be home soon," Nick said, patting his mother's back as though he was the parent and she was the child. "Can I do anything for you?"

She pulled a tissue from the apron pocket and wiped her nose. "No, baby. I'll be all right. I just hate that this is happening here. Things like this happen to other people. In other towns. Not here."

"It's hard to believe," Nick said, wiping at his eyes, which had begun to tear up. "I think I'll go to my room and lay down, if you don't need me."

"Oh, honey. I can imagine how upsetting this must be for you. Go ahead, I'll call you when dad gets home."

Inside his room, with the door closed, Nick lay on the bed and listened to the rain sluicing through the trees, splashing loudly off the roof of their porch. Thunder rumbled in the distance and he thought they were in for one of those storms that would bludgeon them for most of the night before moving off shore. He got up and went to his desk in the corner of the small room. On the walls were a few posters, one of Taylor Swift, and a black and white poster from a marathon race of a single runner in full stride approaching the finish line.

The desk had two drawers on one side. An iMac computer sat alone on the pristine desk. A bookshelf held several dozen books, neatly squared away, their spines lined up like little soldiers. He sat in the swivel chair, propped one foot against the top drawer, thinking about what had happened this afternoon. Nick picked up the iPhone and wondered again if April had really texted him. If so, why hadn't she followed up after he learned Kelly didn't know who killed her?

He heard the front door open and close. His father was home. It was going to be one of those depressing nights, and he wasn't sure he was ready for it. There was a knock on his bedroom door.

"Nick, are you okay, buddy?" His father sounded concerned.

"I guess so."

"Well, how about some dinner?"

"I'm not very hungry, dad. Do you mind if I just skip it tonight and do some homework? Maybe I'll grab a sandwich later."

Everything was quiet for a while, then he heard whispers outside his door before his mother said, "Sure, honey. This has upset all of us. We can talk later."

He listened to them walk away, and heard the hushed voices of his parents in the kitchen. Maybe his mother was telling his father that the neighborhood was too dangerous. That they should sell the house and move to the other side of town. That might be the best thing for everyone. He'd miss his school and competing in the cross country races, but there were other schools and other teams.

He listened for a few more minutes and heard the familiar sounds of a meal being served and eaten. Nick looked over to be sure the door was locked before moving his foot and pulling the desk drawer out. He tilted it up, lifted the entire drawer from the runners, and set it on the bed. Taped to the back of the drawer was a slim plastic box about five by seven inches. It had originally held a collector's set of six GI Joe figures he'd received as a birthday gift when he turned ten, the same year his dog was killed. He thought he still had the figures somewhere in his closet.

Nick crossed to the wicker clothes hamper his mother had bought for his room. Inside, he dug out the pair of muddy shorts he'd worn on his run and fished something out of the pocket. Holding it up, he watched the light reflecting off the stone and cheap silvertone finish. The kids called it a mood ring, and it had been a yellowish-greenish color when he found it, but now it had turned a dark blue, almost black.

Nick smiled at the little trinket and returned to his bed. He freed the plastic case from the back of the drawer, opened it, and looked at the charm bracelet nestled inside next to an earring, a skull and cross bones ring, and a dog collar. He spent some time with each of them, reliving pleasant memories, before tucking them all into the box and taping it to the back of the drawer again.

After he had replaced the drawer, he sat back in his chair, his hands folded behind his head. It really had been an extraordinary day. The text messages from April led him right to Kelly. He smiled as he recalled his visit with her.

His thoughts were interrupted by the chiming of his phone. Another text. Nick studied the screen. Could it be, he wondered? Could this possibly be a message from Kelly?

THE THIRD WHISPER

From time to time I've read news accounts of bank employees forced to rob their own banks. In 2012, a Los Angeles bank manager was abducted and a device strapped to her body. She was told it was a bomb and it would detonate if she didn't do as they say. The kidnappers drove her to the bank and in fear of her life she gathered all the money she could and threw it into the parking lot where the waiting thieves escaped with the loot. As it turned out, the device was harmless.

There have been other such daring robberies, some of them involved holding the bank manager's family hostage. It must have been one of these news stories that triggered the initial idea for *Wimmer's Luck*. Never having been a banker or the victim of kidnappers, I dipped into my writer's toolbox for the premise, used my imagination to create the four characters—the good guys and the bad guys—and tried to imagine the mounting terror of the situation. I wondered what impact it might have not only on the banker, Bonnie Wimmer, but her husband, poor Mr. Wimmer who was held prisoner while his wife was forced to pillage her bank's vault of several million dollars.

We might consider ourselves a civilized people, but every day we read of acts of violence and savagery. Fear and paranoia lurk very near the surface, and who can say how any of us would react in a situation like the one that faced Mr. Wimmer.

Now it's time for you to see if Wimmer's luck holds out.

wimmer's luck

Wimmer's Luck

Rough hands pushed Wimmer's head down and guided him through the car's door into the rear seat.

"Keep going," ordered a voice that sounded like it had been scraped raw by a rusty hacksaw blade.

Blindfolded, with his hands bound, Wimmer squatted between the front and back seats. He held his breath and waited.

"I hope you're not too uncomfortable back there."

This was a different voice belonging to the man who called himself Ted who must have been sitting in the driver's seat. The other intruder, the one Ted referred to as Ed, and who looked like he had been carved out of a mountain of coal, had been the one who pushed him into the back seat.

The car shifted under Ed's enormous bulk as he settled into the passenger seat. Wimmer felt like the victim of a mine collapse, trapped in a dark, claustrophobic hole, unable to move. Ed had slapped a strip of duct tape over his mouth, adding to his claustrophobia. A loud sigh emerged from deep inside Wimmer's throat and emerged as a gargled groan through sealed lips.

"Are you all right?" Ted asked.

This time his voice came from directly over his head. Wimmer envisioned Ted leaning over the front seat, talking down to him the way you'd berate a small child or a puppy that had peed on the carpet.

Wimmer grunted into his tape and nodded.

"This will be over soon. In a half-hour we'll all have what we want. We get our money and you have your freedom. Now relax and we'll get going."

With those words, the car door slammed and the engine started. Wimmer's heart pounded in his chest, a spike of adrenaline thrusting the damaged organ into overdrive. He thought he heard it beating, picking up speed like an overloaded steam engine, pistons pumping dangerously, and threatening to explode through the thick red scar bisecting his chest.

If anything, it was his imagination that was in overdrive. The only sound he heard was the *thrum* of the motor, the vibrations zinging through the chassis and tickling his cheek. He caught the pungent odor of cigarettes, stale French fries and burgers, and wondered if the pair had been living in this vehicle.

A cramp seared a path up the back of his ankle into his calf. He shifted his weight to relieve the pain. With the pain easing, Wimmer thought of Bonnie, his wife. He couldn't imagine the pressure she must be feeling. She had to go about her job like it was just another day at the bank, not let on that anything was wrong.

She called in every hour as Ted had instructed, and Wimmer was allowed to whisper a few words of encouragement to Bonnie, assuring her he was still alive.

Only minutes had passed since her last telephone call, so he knew it must be about 4:35.

A picture of the digital display on the front of Bonnie's bank came to mind, flashing the time and temperature. Throughout the day, he had tried to imagine what would happen when the time came to make this ride to the bank. How would he feel when the ordeal was finally over, and Ted and Ed drove out of their lives?

Wimmer thought again about the bank's clock flashing the time, letting his mind drift back to last night, the time before their lives had been turned upside down. The evening had started off pleasantly enough. They'd eaten dinner at Joseppi's, one of their favorite restaurants, and he had suggested taking a cruise to celebrate their 10th anniversary in October. Bonnie wasn't sure she could get away, but she left the door open and Wimmer didn't press the matter.

He went to bed at around 11:00, and found Bonnie already asleep, her back to him, sheet pulled to her shoulders. More times than not these days she was asleep by the time he got to bed. Since his heart attack and by-pass surgery, he had difficulty sleeping. The doctor had prescribed medication, but the pills gave him crazy dreams and left him feeling dizzy and weak so he stopped taking them.

Each morning, Bonnie was up at 5:00 a.m. and off to the bank by 6:30. She'd been working long hours, and Wimmer realized he hadn't given her much reason to stay awake in the months since his heart attack.

He tried to put those memories aside and thought about how their lives had suddenly changed abruptly at 4:15 a.m. when Wimmer felt something hard prodding his right temple.

He'd finally fallen asleep after tossing and turning for hours, and he remembered brushing at his head, thinking that something—there were plenty of bugs in South Florida—something must be crawling over his face. He didn't find any bugs. Instead a hand yanked him up by the arm and pressed the barrel of a gun into his head.

Stray wisps of moonlight filtered in from the slatted blinds and he managed a fleeting glimpse of a huge, hard-faced dark man in a gray hooded sweatshirt.

"Don't do anything foolish, Mr. Wimmer. Cooperate with us and neither of you will get hurt."

The voice came from the other side of the bed. Bonnie's side. Wimmer recognized the man's Brooklyn accent—he had dropped the *r* in his name so it sounded like *Wimmah*.

Wimmer attempted to swing his legs out from under the covers and stand, to push the gun away. The hooded man shoved him against the mahogany headboard and prodded him painfully in the ear with the pistol.

Wimmer froze, cutting his eyes toward his wife's side of the bed. She was sitting up, her back pressed against a shadowy figure holding a gloved hand over her mouth and a gun to her head. His sweet Bonnie, her lovely green eyes wide with panic, was silently pleading with him to do something. The gun nudged him again.

"Okay, okay," Wimmer blurted out. "We'll cooperate, just don't hurt my wife."

"That's a good boy," said the voice belonging to the man who later introduced himself as Ted. "Close your eyes and don't say another word. Do you understand?"

"Yes."

"Good. In case you think this is a big game, let me warn you not to try anything, or my friend here will blow a hole through your head."

Wimmer started to say he wouldn't try anything, but before he could the huge, dark man slapped a piece of duct tape over his mouth. Moments later, a black cloth was wrapped around his head, completely covering his eyes. Jerked forward onto his stomach, Wimmer's arms were forced behind his back and his wrists securely tied.

"Now we can get down to business. It's dark, you can't identify us, so unless you screw up, there's no reason to take permanent measures. Understand what I'm saying?"

Wimmer nodded his agreement without any prompting. He wanted to cooperate and get this thing over with, and hoped that Bonnie would do the same. He knew how headstrong his wife could be, but she must understand these men would kill them if they didn't do as they were told.

"Your first name's Bonnie, right?" the voice cut through his thoughts. "Well, Bonnie, you and I are going to have a little talk. I'll take my hand away, but if you try to scream or give us any trouble, you and your husband are in for some real pain. Nod if you feel you're ready to listen."

Behind his blindfold, Wimmer couldn't see Bonnie's reaction. Couldn't see if she would take a chance that they were bluffing and scream her head off.

She must have nodded because the man said, "That's a smart girl, Bonnie. And to show you we're stand-up guys, you can call me Ted. The man babysitting your husband is Ed. We're what you might call entrepreneurs, and we have a deal to offer you."

Wimmer heard nothing from his wife, and Ted continued. "We've done our homework, Bonnie. We know you're the manager of the Worth Avenue branch of Gulfstream Bank. And your bank usually has around five hundred thousand dollars in cash on hand. Right?"

Wimmer listened to the silence and knew his wife was calculating the odds of telling Ted the truth, trying to determine how much he really knew about her business. Finally, she said, "Yes, that's about right, but—"

Ted cut her off. "But today they'll be dropping off two million dollars to cover your commercial clients' payrolls. Ain't that what you were about to say?"

"How do you …" Bonnie's voice trailed off.

"How do I know about the delivery? You'd be surprised what I know, Bonnie. I know that the time release on the vault opens at seven-fifteen a.m. That you and several of your employees will already be there, preparing the teller stations for the eight a.m. opening. I know that Wells Fargo will be coming in at four-fifteen p.m., right before your four-thirty closing."

Ted paused and Wimmer tried to imagine what was going through his wife's head. Bonnie may be frightened and confused, but she had a first class mind. Right now, her mind was working its way through the security procedures, considering the possibilities of alerting the police or her home office. She might be wondering if their lives were really in danger, and how far she could push these men before they pushed back.

"And after they deliver the money, we know you'll personally inventory it before you lock the vault for the night."

"Yes, but I won't be alone. We have strict procedures and one of the other employees will be there with me."

"You mean that Clarkson guy, your Trust Officer? Yeah, sometimes you and Clarkson are alone in that vault after hours counting money, and …" he hesitated for a beat. "And doing other stuff."

There was a note of crude innuendo in Ted's tone that bothered Wimmer.

"And sometimes he leaves early and you lock the vault yourself."

"I don't see how you could possibly know that," Bonnie said stiffly.

"I told you we've been watching you. Not only from outside the bank, but we have someone inside the bank keeping an eye on everything you do."

"You're bluffing. None of my people would do that."

Wimmer heard the determination in her voice, but there was also a hint of doubt. He knew his wife well enough to realize she was mentally reviewing each of her employees to see if any of them had acted strangely in the past few months.

"I'm not a bluffing kind of guy, Bonnie, as you'll find out if you don't cooperate with us. Now here's what you're going to do: After you send the truck on its way, and the bank closes at four-thirty, you tell everyone bye-bye, including Mr. Clarkson. Then it's just you and all that money."

"But we're not allowed to be alone with an open vault," Bonnie said.

"You don't give yourself enough credit. You're a bank officer. Been there, what, fifteen, sixteen years? They trust you to do the right thing. If anyone asks, you tell them you're double-checking the deposit, and will be leaving soon. Is that clear?"

"I can't do that."

Wimmer heard a shriek of pain from his wife and twisted around trying to move toward her. Ed pushed him back on the bed, held him there with one massive hand.

"Why'd you make me do that, Bonnie? We was getting along so good. Remember, the bank is covered. The money is insured and they'll get it back. But you and your hubby only have one life. You won't get those back if you don't follow the plan."

"There's no way—"

A sharp intake of breath was followed by a gasp of pain. She sobbed and Wimmer yelled into his gag, but only a series of feral grunts emerged. He wanted to tell Ted not to hurt her. Stop whatever he was doing to Bonnie— pulling her hair, twisting her arm, maybe things he was afraid to imagine.

"This doesn't have to go down this way. Can't you see you're upsetting Mr. Wimmer? And what do you get out of it but more bruises?" Ted's voice had taken on a pedantic tone as though he were a professor lecturing a class of dim-witted freshmen. "Listen to me, Bonnie, and listen good. This is going to be a regular workday for you. You're going to put on one of your pretty dresses, go to the bank, and stick to your regular schedule. Are you with me so far?

"Yes."

"I'm going to give you a cell phone. At eight-thirty, you'll call home. Then I want to hear from you every hour after that. If you're more than two minutes late with that call, for whatever reason, your husband dies. If you call the police or your supervisors, your husband dies. Get the picture?"

"I'll do what you say." The words came out between intakes of breath as though she'd been running.

"You say that, but maybe you're thinking your old man here has seen better days, and probably doesn't have much time left, anyway. So you can afford to take a chance.

"No, I wouldn't—"

"But you, on the other hand, Bonnie, still have a lotta years left. You're easy on the eyes, and can probably find another husband. If that's what you're thinking, and you want to call my bluff, ask yourself how much your own life is worth."

More than anything, Wimmer longed to see his wife's face, to understand what she was feeling at this moment. He hoped she was paying close attention, and understood these men had the upper hand.

"When you leave the house, you better remember everything I tell you. You'll hafta act like it's just another day at the office. We'll know if you do anything suspicious. If you get any unplanned visits from the police, for instance."

"I wouldn't do that."

"But if you did we'd know, and that would be the end of both of you. And believe me, it won't be pretty. My friend Ed here might not talk much, but he has a certain reputation with the ladies. I'm sure he would appreciate spending a little personal time with you, if you get my meaning."

Wheels bucking over railroad tracks brought Wimmer back to the present. Must be the tracks at Atlantic Boulevard he thought. That means we're about halfway to the bank. Close to bringing this crazy day to an end. He calculated that if the traffic wasn't too heavy and they caught the lights, they should be there in fifteen minutes. Fifteen minutes until they get their cash.

That was the plan Ted had recounted to Bonnie some twelve hours ago. He'd told her to take the deposit out of the vault after everyone left, and then to lock it the way she did every night. Ted said that he would call her cell when they arrived at 5:00 o'clock.

At 6:30 a.m. Bonnie left with the cell phone Ted had given her. The first call came in at exactly 8:30 as Ted had instructed. He answered and assured her that everything would be fine if she continued following the plan. Then he passed the phone to Wimmer.

"Bonnie, are you all right?" he croaked into the phone. Wimmer listened for a moment before telling her, "Yes, baby, I'm fine. Don't worry about me, just do everything they say and we'll—"

Ted snatched the phone from Wimmer's hand. "That's all the sweet talk for now," he told her. "Go back to work and call again at nine-thirty. Don't forget that we're watching you."

Wimmer had plenty of time to think between phone calls. He remembered the day that he and Bonnie had met. His rocky twelve-year marriage had recently come to an end, and Wimmer had made a vow of celibacy. He was determined to put all of the painful memories and distractions behind him. From now on, he told himself, work would be his mistress.

His resolve left him the day he met Bonnie Wallace. He'd never met any woman with such a combination of smarts, self-confidence and good looks. At first, he felt a bit like a lovesick schoolboy smitten for the first time. He waited for the feeling to pass, knowing in his heart that it would never work between them. She was at least a dozen years younger than him, and Wimmer couldn't imagine someone like Bonnie attracted to a much older man, even though he was only forty-eight.

But amazing things happen in life. What was it that one of his boyhood friends liked to call it, "the urge to merge?" The urge was certainly there, and despite all logic, the two of them were drawn together. They were married after a brief courtship.

That was ten years ago. Since then, Bonnie had moved from loan officer to commercial banking to vice president and manager of the Worth Avenue branch which was the largest and most prestigious next to the downtown home office. Wimmer, who had been head of international banking for Gulfstream, became a senior vice president and oversaw the operations of several branches, including Bonnie's. Many in the company felt he was on a fast track to move into the president's office, but his career train caromed off the track when his heart failed him last year.

The car braked suddenly and the sound of a car horn interrupted Wimmer's thoughts.

"Damn people don't know how to drive in this town. If it was up to me, I'd slice this rotten state in half and let it sink," Ted said.

"Uh huh," Ed mumbled.

"Lousy heat and humidity. Why the hell do you want to live down here, Wimmer? Most people can't even speak English."

For the first time, Ted sounded impatient. The stress must be getting to him, too, Wimmer figured.

Again he thought of Bonnie and the horrible stress she must be feeling. By her fourth telephone call at 11:30 that morning, Wimmer heard the increased tension in her voice and wondered if she'd make it to the bank's closing.

"Bonnie, you have to hang in there," he'd said when Ted put the phone to his ear.

"Yes, I know," she answered in a muted voice as though she was afraid someone might overhear her. "What about you? They're not hurting you, are they?"

"I'm fine baby. Believe me this will be over before you know it. Do what they say and I'll see you soon."

"I'm not sure I can do this." Bonnie's voice cracked, and Wimmer's heartbeat jumped at the thought of what would happen if she didn't follow the plan.

"Bonnie, listen to me, these men are serious and if we don't do exactly as they say—"

Ted yanked the phone from his hand. "Listen to your husband, Mrs. Wimmer. There are only five hours left before your last call and we'll be rolling out of your life right after that. You'll never see us again."

With luck, Wimmer told himself, everything would work out fine. And he'd always considered himself lucky. Aside from the nightmare divorce from his last wife, an experience that had him swearing off women forever, and his heart attack, most things had eventually gone his way.

Wimmer had come a long way from his childhood where it seemed the only luck anyone had was bad. He'd grown up in a New York hellhole with a drunken father and a mother who had run off when he was five. Half of the kids on his block were either dead or in prison. Wimmer was on a path to follow his friends, but a lucky encounter with a judge who saw potential in the boy and sent him to a school for bright but troubled youth changed his life. Instead of doing drugs and joining a gang, Wimmer earned scholarships first to a prestigious prep school and later to an Ivy League college.

Yes, luck had a lot to do with it, Wimmer thought. Hard work, too. He rose through the ranks at the Bank of New England, survived two mergers and moved to South Florida to work for Gulfstream. All so lucky, but when Bonnie agreed to marry him, he thought he was the luckiest man in the world.

The heart attack changed everything. It turned him into an invalid overnight. The coronary had been so massive they didn't think he'd survive. He guessed luck may have played a part in keeping him alive, but in those first six weeks when he was filled with anger and self-pity, he railed at his luck and wished he'd died on the operating table.

Bonnie had taken a month off to care for him, but then returned to work and buried herself in her job. She'd always been a conscientious worker, but now she seemed driven by some furious inner ambition to climb the corporate ladder. Soon she was working longer and longer days. Not getting home until after 8:00, blaming meetings with clients, and planning sessions at the home office. In the past year, she'd even gone away for weekend conferences a few times, something she'd never done before.

At home Bonnie no longer crackled with energy, but often went to bed early, leaving him to watch television or read alone. He couldn't blame her. Since his heart attack, he wasn't the same person.

Surely, a half-hour had passed since they left the house, Wimmer thought. He'd made this drive many times in the past; dropping Bonnie off at work on his way downtown, sometimes picking her up after work, and waiting for her to lock the vault. He thought he could have made the drive blindfolded. Funny, now he was blindfolded and picturing the route in his head.

"There's the bank." Ted sounded excited.

The vehicle slowed, and Wimmer felt a slight bump.

We're in the bank parking lot.

The plan called for them to park next to the employee entrance on the west side of the bank next to a solid steel door that was all but hidden by a high hedge and could only be accessed with an employee code. The car stopped, although the engine kept running.

"We're outside," Ted said, and Wimmer realized he must have called Bonnie's cell phone. Moments later, both of the car's front doors opened, and Wimmer heard the trunk lid pop behind him.

She must have the money.

"Hurry. You take three bags and I'll take the other two." Ted's muffled voice floated in through the open doors. This was followed by the thump of sacks flung into the trunk and the slamming of the lid.

The passenger door closed and Wimmer caught a whiff of Bonnie's perfume.

She's here.

Next the back door opened and the springs groaned in protest.

That's the mountain man, Ed. He's moved into the back seat.

"Buckle up, Mrs. Wimmer. Can't have anything happen to you at this point." The car accelerated and they drove away from the bank.

"Where's my husband? Where's Frank?" Wimmer heard the ragged edge of panic insinuating itself into her voice as she fought to retain control.

"Not to worry. He's resting on the floor behind you," Ted answered.

Bonnie must have twisted in her seat, because Wimmer felt her hand slide across his back. "Can't you let him sit up? He's not a well man, and he must be terribly uncomfortable down there."

"Hmm. What about it, Mr. Wimmer? Can we trust you to be a good boy if we let you up?"

The bastard is really enjoying this.

Wimmer grunted through his gag.

"I guess that's a yes. Ed, take the tape and blindfold off before you lift him up. We can't have anyone seeing him like that and calling the police. But leave his hands tied."

Sunlight poured over Wimmer, blinding him for a moment. Before he could react to the sudden removal of his blindfold, Ed grasped the edge of the duct tape covering his mouth and snatched it off with a single pull. Wimmer let out a sharp gasp of pain and shot a nasty look at Ed who ignored him.

Bonnie watched as he was lifted from the floor and guided back onto the seat, her eyes wide, and a look of relief on her face.

"Feel better?" Ted asked.

Wimmer rolled his head around a few times trying to loosen the kink in his neck. "Yes, much better. Thank you."

"Settle back and relax. We're going for a drive in the country."

They drove west for nearly forty-five minutes, carefully observing the speed limit and stopping at every yellow light. Wimmer recognized one of the roads as State Road 704, and they passed Haverhill and Loxahatchee. After numerous turns, he'd lost his bearings, but he suspected they might be nearing Lake Okeechobee. A weed-filled canal ran along one side of the road while a vast panorama of sawgrass, palm hammocks and white mangrove stretched to the horizon on the other side.

After another fifteen minutes, Ted turned onto a rutted dirt road that seemed to float atop the swamp, and they bounced along until all signs of life had disappeared. Deep into the swamp, on the edge of a stand of scrub pines, Ted stopped the car next to a barren shack.

"Where ... where are we?" Bonnie asked, taking in the shack with horrified eyes.

She turned to Ted. "You said you'd let us go after you got the money. You can't leave us out here. We'll never find our way back."

"Don't you worry your pretty little head about it, Mrs. Wimmer. We're just taking a rest stop." He came around to the passenger side and pulled Bonnie out of the car. "Ed, I suspect Mr. Wimmer might need your help."

Ed opened the door and placed a hand under Wimmer's arm, easing him out of the car. It felt like the bones in his legs had liquefied, and he nearly collapsed, but Ed supported him with more gentleness than Wimmer would have thought possible.

The outside of the shack hadn't seen a coat of paint in decades, if ever. The door was askew, windows boarded over. Ted scraped the door open and stood aside while Bonnie and then Wimmer entered. A wall of heat hit them along with the smell of decay from an animal that had crawled in the shack and never left.

Ted fumbled around in the dark and soon a warm light illuminated the room. From the light of a camping lantern sitting atop a heavy wooden table, Wimmer spotted a pair of palmetto bugs as long as his index finger resting on the table. Ted slapped the table and the bugs disappeared into the shadows.

Two folding camp chairs sat at opposite corners of the table. "Have a seat,"

Ted told them.

When they were seated, Ted grabbed Bonnie's right wrist, wrapped a plastic tie around it, interlocked it with another, and attached it to the table leg.

"That's not necessary," Bonnie protested. "Where can we go?"

"Nowhere. That's the point. Now sit tight while we get the money. I want to make sure you didn't pull a fast one on us."

Wimmer waited until both men had left the shack before whispering to his wife. "Bonnie, did you bring them all the money like they asked?"

She cut her eyes toward the door and back. "Yes. It's all there. I did everything they asked."

"Good."

"Do you think they're really going to let us go? I'm scared."

"They got what they wanted—the money. So I guess we have to trust them to keep their word."

Ed muscled his way through the open door carrying three large brown canvas courier bags. Ted followed with two more sacks. They dropped them on the table and Ted rubbed his hands together like a young boy anticipating Christmas morning.

"Did you count it yourself?" he asked Bonnie.

"It's all there—two million, two-hundred and fifty thousand dollars."

Ted's eyes sparkled and he prodded his partner jubilantly on the shoulder. He might as well have shoved the Washington Monument for all the good it did. The huge man didn't budge.

"Ed, we got ourselves an extra qua-ta-milyon," he said excitedly, his Brooklyn accent becoming more pronounced. "That's an unexpected bonus."

He picked up one of the bags, which, like the others, had a molded plastic bottom, and a leather trim surrounding the top with a strap running through brass grommets. Ted pulled the strap through the grommets and pried the bag open. He stared into the bag and inhaled, a broad smile spreading over his face. "Man, there's nothing like that new-cash smell."

Ted grabbed the bottom of the bag, turning it over, and spilling the bundles of bills across the table. He looked at Bonnie and asked, "Is the two million split equally in the five bags."

"Two million, two-hundred and fifty thousand," she corrected. "And yes, there's four-hundred and fifty thousand in each sack."

Ted picked up one of the bundles of bills. "And how much in each of these bundles?"

"Five thousand dollars," Bonnie said.

"Five thousand. Good," he said, riffling through the bills. "Good," he repeated.

As Bonnie and her husband watched, Ted placed five bundles of cash in a row in front of him. He repeated the process adding another layer to each stack, mumbling to himself and tapping a finger against each pile, obviously calculating the total as he distributed the bundles.

Wimmer had a brief image of the Great Wall of China, someplace he'd always wanted to visit, and pictured the cash snaking around the table like the Wall. But after three more layers, Ted stepped back and admired his handiwork.

Ted turned to Bonnie who had been watching closely. "That's one-hundred thousand, right?" Ted said.

"Yes," Bonnie replied.

"Good. That's makes it even-Steven." With that, Ted scooped up the remainder of the money and returned it to the bag, leaving the wall of $100 bills lined up across one side of the table. He placed the bag on the floor by his feet and pulled another one up, removed the strap and examined the contents. Obviously satisfied, he repeated the process with the other three bags.

Throughout this inspection, Ed stood motionless between Wimmer and Bonnie, watching with narrowed eyes as Ted examined each pouch, and moved on to the next.

When he'd completed his appraisal, Ted said, "S'all here. Now let's divvy it up." He pushed two of the full courier bags over to the $100,000 line of currency he had counted out first.

"One million dollars," Ted said under his breath. He smiled at Bonnie before glancing up at his partner.

As if an invisible signal had passed between them, Ed pulled a six-inch folding knife from his pocket. Bonnie watched in horror as the brutish man she knew only as Ed flicked the knife open, its blade glittering in the lantern light, and silently moved behind her husband. He thrust his ape-like arms down, the knife hand disappearing for a moment.

"No, no," she screamed. "I got you the money. You can't …"

Her voice cracked and she gasped for breath. She dropped her head, sobbing wildly, unable to watch what was happening, waiting to hear her husband's dying scream.

Laughter greeted her instead. Slowly, she opened her eyes and lifted her head. Her husband leaned against the table, holding the rope that had been knotted around his wrists. Wimmer twirled the rope lazily once, twice, and then let it drop onto the table next to one of the courier bags stuffed with $450,000.

"Frank, thank God you're all right," Bonnie cried.

Wimmer saw relief wash over her face, and was that a … yes, it was a tear forming in her eye.

"I'm fine, Bonnie. Thank you for your concern. Other than the uncomfortable ride to your bank, everything's gone as planned."

Bonnie's mouth sagged open slightly and she looked from Wimmer to Ted to Ed and back to Wimmer in confusion. "But … but, I don't understand," she stammered.

"It's simple, my dear. You've helped us pull off the perfect crime." He turned to Ted and with a slight tip of his head said, "You may remember my rags to riches stories of growing up in the Bronx. Well, Ted here is one of my childhood buddies. In a way, we both ended up in the banking business, although Ted is known more for his withdrawals than deposits."

Ted laughed, and Bonnie's jaw dropped another inch before she swallowed and spit out one word. "Why?"

Wimmer thought the lantern light didn't do her justice, adding years to her age. "That's a fair question, but you probably already know the answer." He waited for a reply and when none came he continued.

"Infidelity is the one thing I can never forgive. Not after my last marriage, and—"

"No, I'd never do that," Bonnie blurted out.

"Ah, but you would, and you did. Don't try to deny it. I have the proof. After your routine changed and you began coming home later and later, even leaving me alone for *weekend conferences*," he said sarcastically, "I hired a private investigator."

Bonnie's face hardened as she shot icy beams of hate toward him.

"He was quite good and brought me rather lurid photographs of you and your trusted vice associate, Bruce Clarkson, in some rather compromising positions. I'd show them to you, but we really don't have much time. To be accurate, I should say that you don't have much time."

She shook her head defiantly. "You can't expect to get away with this. What are you going to say when they discover the money is gone, and you're alive and I'm not?"

Wimmer smiled at his wife. "Since you asked, I'll tell you. Ted is going to return me to our house. Eventually, I'll free myself, remove my gag and call the police. I'll explain how we were the victims of a home invasion, and how they forced you to take the money from the vault."

He paused and moved to his wife and gently touched her soft blond hair that often smelled of freshly sliced peaches after she'd showered.

"You left for work this morning, and regrettably, that was the last time I saw you. And after you took the money from the vault, you disappeared along with Ted and Ed."

"Maybe you can make me disappear, but that much money is hard to hide."

Wimmer pursed his lips and seemed to consider her statement for a moment. "I know it's been a long time since I worked, but don't forget that I made my living moving money around the world." He pointed to the cash on the table. "All of this will soon be in several Swiss bank accounts where no one will ever find it. Of course, they will find one smaller account in the Bahamas that I set up for you and Bruce."

Terror filled Bonnie's eyes as she understood the implications of his words. "No, you can't do this." She thrashed wildly, pulling at her restraint until her chair slipped out from beneath her and she dropped to her knees still secured to the heavy old table.

"You can take comfort in knowing that to the police, you'll be very much alive. And an international fugitive, I might add. Poor Bruce will probably be jailed for his unwitting part in your daring robbery."

Wimmer nodded to Ed who grabbed the three courier bags on the floor and carried them outside. Ted opened the other two bags and stuffed the additional $100,000 into them, handing them to Ed when he returned.

"Be careful with my million, please," Wimmer said.

"After a few months to get over your rude departure, I may even go back to work. Or maybe I'll be a high-paid consultant for a few years before retiring and enjoying the fruits of my labor."

Still on her knees, tears flowed down Bonnie's cheeks. Wimmer tried to dredge up a bit of compassion for his wife, to recall the good times they'd shared, but all he found in his memory were the graphic color photos the detective had given him. He turned when he heard the car's trunk slam shut and watched as Ted and Ed reentered the shack.

"Time to go," Ted said.

Ed moved to stand beside Wimmer's sobbing wife.

"I'm afraid I'll have to leave you here with Ed," Wimmer said and walked away without looking back.

Wimmer stood in the open door looking out at the sun setting behind the pine trees. He inhaled the warm summer air, heavy with the pungent smells of the surrounding marsh. God, it was good to be alive. Good to have a fresh start.

Before he joined Ted in the car, he took one last look at the shack, and felt a twinge of sorrow. He was sorry it hadn't worked out between them. Sorry for

Bonnie, whose muffled groans he heard rolling out of the shack. But then, it wasn't his fault she had cheated on him. He thought of the million dollars that would help him overcome his sorrow and realized that getting caught was her bad luck and his good fortune.

Wimmer climbed into the passenger seat thinking he would miss his wife, but not for long. There was all that money to spend and other women to console him. After his last disastrous marriage, Wimmer had sworn off women. Not this time. Deep in his heart he knew that somewhere there was a woman who would love and cherish him until death parted them.

With luck, he would find her.

THE FOURTH WHISPER

It's funny how stories can change and live on over the years. I first wrote *My Brother, My Burden* as an entry in a Halloween flash fiction contest some fifteen years ago. The guidelines called for a limit of 500 words and instructed us to include specific words and phrases like *Frim Fram* and *goblins*.

My Brother, My Burden ended up a winner in the contest, and over the next few years I made minor changes to the story, eliminating *Frim Fram* for one. Later I submitted it for consideration for the Florida Writers Association's first anthology, a collection called *From Our Family to Yours*. This was a fitting theme for a story of two very different brothers. The story, now enhanced by a few hundred words over the original, made the cut and was published in 2008.

My Brother, My Burden is set in New Orleans on one of the scariest nights of the year— All Hallows' Eve. This is a time when children dressed as goblins and vampires terrorize their neighbors and carry home bags of candy, much to the delight of dentists everywhere.

On what should have been a festive Halloween night, Robert and Harv instead discover life often has different plans for us, and they're often filled with more tricks than treats.

my brother, my burden

My Brother, My Burden

Shadows from the raised tombs grabbed at me as I raced past statues of angels guarding the long dead. Taking a shortcut through Lafayette Cemetery on Halloween night might not be the wisest thing to do, but I have to find Harv before he does something stupid.

Harv's my younger brother, you see, and although he's always been a little strange, tonight he snapped. I guess you could say I was responsible for what happened. Not that it's anything new. Harv's always been different, which is why the kids at school pick on him and call him names. More times than not, he comes home blubbering his eyes out, crying about how he hates everyone and wishes they were dead.

I laugh at him and don't take him seriously. But mom wraps him in her big arms, shushing him until he stops crying. She tells him it doesn't matter what other people think or do. "You're a very special boy," she'll say. "One day you'll be famous and make us all proud."

Halloween is Harv's favorite holiday. Maybe because he can act out his fantasies and blend in with the other kids. We didn't have money to buy fancy costumes, but Harv found a ratty hunting coat and cap in a garbage can and announced he was going trick-or-treating dressed as a big game hunter. He taped a piece of pipe to a hunk of wood he cut to look like a rifle stock. Not a bad job, really, but he always was good with his hands.

This afternoon I watched as he put on the coat and hat, grabbed an old pillowcase to hold all the candy he expected to harvest, and got ready to go knocking on doors. But he never got the chance.

He was acting creepy as usual, waving his gun in my face and pretending to shoot my head off. I'd had enough of his foolishness. I yanked the silly rifle from his hands and threw it in the yard. Harv started screaming about how everyone hated him, and he was going to kill himself. He picked up his fake rifle and ran off toward the river.

Mom came out of the house about that time, slapped me across the head, and told me to go find my brother. I know the spot where Harv likes to sit on the edge of the old wharf and watch the barges slip by. That's why I cut through the cemetery on a night so sticky that heat lightning crackled across the sky. Perfect for Halloween, I thought. On Toledano Street I saw ghosts and goblins roaming in packs calling out to each other in excited voices.

Finally, I was at the wharf, straining to see my little brother through the mist descending over the waterfront.

"Harv, where are you?" I yelled, pacing up and down the wharf. "C'mon, Harv, I'm sorry, okay? Let's go trick-or-treating."

I listened for his answer, but the slap of the Mississippi against rotten boards and the mournful wail of an approaching tugboat were the only sounds I heard.

Standing on the edge of the wharf, I called his name over and over. Nothing. I was about to move on when the cloud layer slipped past the full moon for a few seconds. A slash of light from the moon reflected off something floating in the muddy water. I stared into that inky trough, a feeling of dread rising in my throat.

"Harvey!" My scream sounded foreign to my ears, blood-curdling, filled with horror.

As I watched, the form rolled over and I saw a thin arm rise from the river holding a make-believe rifle. I leaped into the water without thinking, splashing toward the shape wearing a ragged old hunting jacket. I was still feet away when the arm slid below the surface. Frantically, I dove toward him, thrashing at the water like it was one of the nightmare monsters roaming the streets of

New Orleans that night.

Please, God, I prayed, *help me save my brother.* At that moment, my fingertips brushed against soggy cloth before slipping away. My arms flailed madly at the spot in the water where I'd felt what I thought must be Harv's old hunting coat. I pushed deeper, my lungs aching, my waterlogged clothes and shoes dragging me down. Accidentally, I opened my mouth and the putrid river water rushed in and into my throat.

I gagged and fought the voice in my head telling me to give up and swim to the surface. Summoning my last reserve of air and energy, I forced myself toward the muddy bottom of the dirty river. Patting the riverbed I felt something round and hard. My fingers skirted over the close-cropped hair, and I realized it was my brother's head. I could feel my ears ringing and my heart racing and knew this was my last chance to save Harv. I grabbed the back of his jacket and kicked toward the surface.

In the hospital later that night, the doctor examined Harv then came out to talk with my mother. "He'll be fine, Mrs. Oswald. Don't you worry."

Together, we watched him sleep. So small in the hospital bed. So still. It had been a close call, but I had saved my brother.

Tears glinted on mom's face when she embraced me and called me her little hero. "Everything happens for a reason, Robert." She put a hand on Harv's head, one arm still wrapped around me.

"We don't know what the good Lord has planned, but I know there's a reason he was spared." She leaned down and kissed him on the forehead. When she straightened, mom looked at me and with a catch in her voice, said, "Believe me, one day, we'll all be reading about your famous brother, Lee Harvey."

THE FIFTH WHISPER

When it was announced that the theme of the 2012 FWA Collections was "My Wheels," the wheels in my head began to turn. The subject matter of all submissions, the guidelines explained, must be about wheels, wheels of any kind from Ferris Wheels to Hot Wheels, from those metaphorical wheels in our head to training wheels. In other words, whatever wheel fit into our story.

Being of the more literal bent, I thought of an automobile tire, and that dark hitchhiker in my mind tossed an image out of a man rolling a flat tire down a deserted road in the middle of the night. That one image was the birth of *And Promises to Keep*, a short, but emotionally charged story of a man on a mission.

Author Julie Compton read all 60 of the stories that had been accepted for publication in FWA's Collection #4, *My Wheels*, and selected her top ten favorites to be placed at the front of the book. *And Promises to Keep* made Julie's Top Ten list and was published in September, 2012.

There's not much more I can say about this story without becoming a spoiler. Instead, I'll let you join Stefan as he rolls that wheel along a country road. Just be careful of the dangerous curve ahead.

and promises to keep

And Promises to Keep

Waves of pain cascaded through Stefan's chest and down his spine. The strain of rolling the SUV's bulky tire for the past two miles had taken its toll, and he needed a break. He stopped abruptly, the tire wobbling, tilting away from him as though the blacktop possessed a magnetic attraction for Japanese tires.

If the damn thing had been fully inflated it wouldn't be so difficult to control. Of course, if it weren't flat the tire would still be on the front end of his Sequoia where it belonged, and he wouldn't be rolling what amounted to a square tire down a deserted two-laner in the dead of night.

Stefan sucked in a lungful of the sticky August air. He listened and wondered what happened to the insectile symphony that had followed him for the first part of his trek. With old growth pine forests on both sides of the county road, he expected to hear the shuffling and skittering of bugs and small animals. He swiped at a mosquito crooning into his ear. At least not all of the forest's creatures had abandoned him.

Stefan stretched, wishing he could sit and rest, but he needed to get back to Jodie. Staring behind him at the white center line fading into the shadows, he thought about leaving Jodie alone, parked on the side of Highway 316. He knew there was little chance of anyone coming along at this time of night. Still, the possibility tormented him.

Frustrated, Stefan kicked at the tire, feeling the rubber compress under his boot. Why didn't he listen when Jodie complained about the balding tires? But he didn't listen. He'd learned to tune her out long ago. This was one time he should have listened, or at least replaced the spare.

Thinking of Robert Frost's poem, he prodded himself to get moving, reciting the words aloud, "Miles to go and promises to keep."

He hauled the tire off the asphalt, fighting through the pain, propelling it forward. Stefan had been down this road hundreds of times, traveling to see his mother in Citra, camping in the Ocala National Forest. He knew the all-night truck stop usually kept a mechanic on duty to service the big rigs rumbling through filled with pulp wood and God knows what. With any luck, the mechanic would be there to plug the tire and he'd return to Jodie.

Stefan needed to get back to her as soon as possible. His stomach burned thinking about some stranger finding Jodie alone in the car. Stefan wiped the ugly images from his mind. He'd promised her she'd be safe locked in the car and he'd be back soon.

"No one's going to bother you, Jodie." He spoke the words in a rush as if trying to convince himself. It was true he hadn't seen another living thing since he'd left the SUV more than an hour ago.

He tried to picture where he was on the narrow two-lane highway. He'd passed the Black Sink Prairie. Ahead of him stretched the Ocala National Forest with thousands of acres of sand pine scrub forest, wetlands and lakes. He and Jodie had camped there after they were first married.

Unbidden, a picture of Jodie from that last camping trip winged into his head. They were inside their small tent. He tried to comfort her, but she refused to be consoled, slapping at his hands. "I hate you," she had screamed. "Why did I listen to you?" She slapped him again, this time across the face.

He remembered he'd told her it was for the best, that they couldn't afford a kid just then. He promised he'd make it up to her. Stefan thought she'd get over it. She never did, and he felt the sting of her palm on his cheek a dozen times over.

He leaned the tire against his hip, and paused to shake out his aching arms. Light from the slender slice of moon twinkled from the reflectors rimming the warning signs lining the sharp curve.

Stefan pressed on, pushing the tire into the curve, still thinking of Jodie and how she'd changed. In a way, he was glad to be alone, enjoying the deep stillness of the woods.

Lost in his thoughts, Stefan didn't hear the approaching vehicle until it was almost too late. The pick-up truck powered into the curve, swerved dangerously close to the shoulder where the warning signs stood guard. Stefan saw the headlights flare over him, heard the screech of brakes, and threw himself to the side of the road, the tire rolling away.

The truck flew by without any indication the driver had seen him.

He lay in the weeds, his heart hammering in his chest. Slowly he stood, expecting his knees to give way, but they held firm. After finding the tire, he muscled it upright and resumed his journey, buoyed by the realization he was nearing the truck stop. Soon he'd be returning to Jodie as he'd promised.

His hands were blistered by the time he limped into the service area. "Thank you, thank you," he murmured when he saw the open mechanic's bay and the young man in coveralls standing by the big red toolbox.

The mechanic quickly found the puncture, and patched it.

"You're not planning on rolling that thing back to your car?" the mechanic asked. "You look terrible, if you don't mind me saying." He pulled a greasy rag from his back pocket and wiped his hands.

"I've got to get back to my wife," Stefan said.

The mechanic shook his head, his shaggy brown hair flipping over his ears. "Tell you what. Go inside and get yourself a cup of coffee. Let me clean up a little and I'll give you a ride."

"I couldn't do that," Stefan said. "You have a job to do."

"I was about to call it a night when you walked in. My replacement is due any minute."

"I don't want to put you to any trouble."

"No trouble at all. I'm going in that direction anyway."

Thirty minutes later the mechanic eased his Ford truck past the Sequoia and parked. Stefan was out the door a moment later heading toward the rear of the truck.

"Sure I can't give you a hand with that?" There wasn't much conviction in the mechanic's weary voice.

Stefan bounced the tire to the ground. "No, you've done enough. Thanks for everything."

He watched the mechanic disappear down the road. Within minutes he'd bolted the tire in place, lowered the SUV to the ground, and removed the jack.

The night hadn't gone the way he planned, but no harm done. Peering in both directions to be sure no vehicles were coming, Stefan unlocked the Sequoia and hoisted the rear lift gate. He moved the long-handled shovel aside and set the jack down next to the shrouded mass lying just where he left it.

He reached out and touched the cold plastic, his fingers caressing the hard form almost lovingly. Stefan leaned forward, his voice a husky whisper. "I'm back just like I promised. Did you miss me, Jodie?"

The Sixth Whisper

The Strange Case of Lord Byron's Lover originally appeared in a collection of speculative fiction titled *The Prometheus Saga*. There was one unifying premise tying the stories together: each of them must include a humanoid probe left behind by aliens to monitor the progress of the human race. Each of the twelve authors was free to interpret how an alien presence would interact with the human condition over the passing centuries. The alien was virtually immortal and could morph into any human form, take on any human identity, either male or female.

Uncertain of a subject for my story, I consulted with my administrative assistant, Google. After a series of random searches, I discovered a fascinating nugget of literary history that sparked my imagination. In June of 1816, poet Percy Bysshe Shelley and his soon-to-be wife, Mary Wollstonecraft Godwin, spent time with the notorious Lord Byron at his rented estate near Lake Geneva. The visit reportedly involved heavy drinking, sexual tensions, and possibly drug use. On one cold, gloomy evening, after Lord Byron read from a book of German ghost stories, he suggested they each write a ghost story to share with the group.

This amazing confluence of creative minds struck me as the perfect background for my Prometheus story, and I took advantage of it for my own dramatic purposes. Some have claimed that Mary Shelley invented the science fiction genre with her Frankenstein novel. She later credited a "waking dream" for the story idea she shared with her fellow writers. Later, now married to the poet Shelley, Mary expanded on her ghost story and wrote *Frankenstein, or, The Modern Prometheus*. The book was published in 1818 to surprising acclaim and has lived on in films and novels.

This was all fascinating stuff, but I still needed to incorporate the alien presence into the story. After reading that Byron brought an entourage of servants with him to Lake Geneva, I turned the alien into one of Byron's servant girls—and his lover. I wouldn't say that this story wrote itself, but it came to life—much like the Frankenstein monster—quickly and mysteriously.

Most of what you will read in *The Strange Case of Lord Byron's Lover* is based on historical fact—except for the parts I made up. But enough about me. Read on as Mary Shelley, writing in her journal, looks back on her tragic life and the strange events that transpired during the summer of 1816.

The Strange Case of
Lord Byron's Lover

Whoever fights monsters should see to it that in the process he does not become a monster. And if you gaze long enough into an abyss, the abyss will gaze back at you.
—Friedrich Nietzsche

The Strange Case of Lord Byron's Lover

Chapter One

My memory isn't what it once was, but my past is written large within these pages. I beg you to indulge me as I recount a series of perplexing events occurring both before and after I wrote the Gothic opus for which I am known. My work achieved popular success, and even the indomitable Sir Walter Scott congratulated me for my "original genius and power of expression."

However, lest you believe the story I'm about to share in the final pages of my journal is a prideful, self-congratulatory boast, let me assure you that I, Mary Shelley, have a far stranger tale to tell than the man-made monster of my fiction. And like the creature dredged from my nightmares, these events haunt me to this day.

The mystery began innocently enough with a summer holiday spent in Lake Geneva with the notorious Lord Byron in the manor house he called Villa Diodati. I recall the manor, though stately and imposing, was cold and dreary during those days of incessant rain in June of 1816. It was the beginning of a wet, ungenial summer, a portent of the unnatural events to follow.

I didn't mind the cramped quarters of our own rented cottage since Lord Byron welcomed us into his spacious villa for much of the time, but the weather was truly depressing—blustery and rainy during the day, freakishly cold at night. As I look back at those days we resided in the village of Cologny, I can see the weather was the least freakish occurrence during our time spent with Lord Byron and his not-so-secret lover.

To this day a rational explanation defies me, but allow me to detail the mystifying incidents of that week, and perhaps someone perusing this journal after my death will come forth with an answer. Or, like me, you may decide something *unhuman* moved among us that summer—and perhaps still does.

As I began with mention of the weather, I should continue that thread of my story. A remarkable servant girl explained the dramatic change in temperature was directly related to the prior year's volcanic eruption in the islands of Indonesia. At the time I dismissed her explanation as preposterous poppycock, but looking back on what transpired, I now think she may have been correct, though how she would have known such a thing is beyond me. But that is at the heart of this mystery, is it not?

Whatever the reason for the peculiar conditions of that summer, we were forced to give up any thoughts of frolicking in the sun or sailing on the lake. Instead we spent our time reading by candlelight in the shadowed rooms of Villa Diodati, or huddled in front of the massive fireplace, drinking wine to excess.

My impetuous sister Claire—she was only a half-sister, truth be told, and half mad at that—convinced us to journey to Switzerland to spend some time with her former lover, George Gordon Noel Byron on the French-Swiss border. Please take note that George was a profligate in every way possible, including his ostentatious name, and I will henceforth refer to him as either Byron or Lord Byron, as he was more popularly known.

Though I was initially opposed to Claire's suggestion, when the deed was finally done I hoped Percy and I could use the holiday as a way to bring some relief to my grieving over the death of our daughter. Percy often exclaimed that I had a gloomy disposition and tended to lose myself in funereal brooding. This may be true, but I blame my father and the dark angel of death who visited us shortly after my birth, snatching my mother from us, leaving his bloody tracks to plague me, and my father to punish me with silent recriminations.

Looking back on my life, I fear death continued to stalk me throughout my 53 years, depositing one heartbreak after another at my doorstep. Sadly I must report losing four of my five children. My half-sister Claire, who instigated our holiday with Lord Byron, later took her own life. Could there be any doubt why I became nearly deranged by the sting of death's frequent visits? And I haven't yet mentioned death's cruelest torment, transforming me into a widow at the age of 24 when my beloved Percy drowned in a boating accident.

Is it any wonder I took to my bed for weeks, and wrote the following in my journal?

How can I not think that some veiled creature is experimenting with my life? Probing the limits of my sanity with cruel intentions by striking down all that I love and hold dear. Sometimes I feel like Job in the belly of the whale, crying out, "Why me, God? Why me?

I remember with crystal clarity the day I met Percy Bysshe Shelley, how our friendship quickly turned to lust and love. I carried Percy's child until the day she was born. We buried her two days later.

But that is all in the distant past. To begin this story, you only need know that some years after my mother's death, father married a woman of prodigious temper and narrow mind. Suffice to say we clashed in many ways, and Percy and I departed London to travel the continent, no certain destination in mind except what might amuse us and lead us to new pleasures and stimulating company. Claire joined us after the death of our daughter.

Lord Byron had impregnated Claire, as he did many women, before tossing her aside. Poor Claire, foolish to the end, believed he would take her back since she was carrying his child. Her delusions came to a head one early morning in Paris where we had rented rooms on a narrow street to the west of *Place de la Bastille*. I recall Percy and I had just finished making love when the door to our bedroom flew open and Claire rushed in, her cheeks flushed with excitement.

"He's going to summer in Lake Geneva," she gushed.

Neither of us bothered to cover ourselves since Claire had seen us both naked before. In fact, to my dismay, Percy confessed he had bedded her several times before taking up with me.

"Claire, for God's sake, you might knock before breaking down our door," I said. "Now tell me exactly who is going to Lake Geneva, though I can probably guess it must be Lord Byron."

"Who else, my dear sister," she replied, bouncing her large derriere on the bed beside me.

"That is news of no interest to us, I'm afraid."

"Don't you see? Lake Geneva is little more than a day's train ride. We were looking to move on, so why not Switzerland?"

I have previously mentioned Claire's unrestrained infatuation with Byron. He was a man of debauched appetites, and a scandalous reputation for romances with both men and women, including a shameful affair with Augusta, his half-sister. Even among those of us who professed to believe in free love, his behavior was shocking, and I could envision nothing but vexation for my sister.

"Claire, I don't believe a reunion with your former lover is a good idea."

I was trying to be gentle with her, and thought Percy would take my side. Surprisingly, he was anxious to meet Byron. And so we traveled through abnormal wintry conditions to Lake Geneva where Byron and Percy struck up an instant friendship.

Though the three of us rented a modest cottage not far from Villa Diodati, we were soon introduced to the manor and its amazing inhabitants. With Byron's arrival, the villa transformed into an elegant carnival tent stocked with his coterie of servants, assorted sycophants, and his personal physician, Dr. John Polidori, who was darkly handsome and overly flirtatious. Along with Byron's excessive staff, he'd also brought along a menagerie of eight dogs, three monkeys, five cats, an eagle, a crow, and a peacock, as well as horses for the splendid Napoleonic coach he'd had built to transport him in the style he believed a lord should enjoy. Percy would complain that the villa was more of a zoo since all of the animals, except the horses, were free to walk around the house.

And then there was Anastasia.

Anastasia was the remarkable servant girl I alluded to earlier in my narrative. Remember her name, for it is she who stands at the center of the mystery surrounding our time spent with Lord Byron. At first blush, the girl seemed like nothing more than what she appeared to be, one of the retinue of servants Byron had carried with him to cater to his every whim during his summer sojourn to escape the creditors and notoriety he'd left behind in London.

It soon became clear Anastasia serviced Byron in many ways, including helping to satiate his ravenous sexual appetites. I understood why a man like Lord Byron would be drawn to this young girl of Greek descent. She was 23 or 24 years of age, with the coloring and dark hair of the Mediterranean people. Anastasia was attractive, though she didn't strike me as beautiful. But there was an allure to her, a sexual magnetism that clung to her like a second skin.

I was instantly struck by the boldness of her gaze and the exceptional shine of her dark eyes, which sometimes seemed to glow with an otherworldly light. She listened more than she spoke, an agreeable trait for a young woman of her breeding, often with her head slightly canted to one side like a curious hound. When she did speak, however, her utterances were most astonishing, as you will soon see.

Lord Byron turned out to be as charming as he was exceedingly handsome, and I could see why so many young women (and apparently, boys) had fallen under his spell. After his affair with Lady Caroline Lamb, she publically described Byron as "mad, bad, and dangerous to know." I believe he took Lady Lamb's portrayal as a badge of honor, and worked hard to live up to it.

Lord Byron was proud of the two-story manor he'd rented, and soon after we had settled into our simple abode near the lakefront, he arranged a tour of Villa Diodati. Byron himself escorted us through the first floor, commenting on the paintings and sculptures throughout the living areas, the exceptionally fine library and grand ballroom, but he left it to Anastasia to guide us through the upper story.

We all knew Byron was sensitive about his malformed foot. I personally felt he was overly sensitive, as we paid little heed to his impediment, which was vastly overshadowed by his genius. Even so, he seemed loath to lead us up the stairs in those preternaturally darkened conditions for fear he might stumble or appear ungainly, I supposed.

Anastasia had followed us through the first part of the tour, hanging at a distance, as was sometimes her habit when Byron was on the move, as though she might be summoned to fulfill some duty for her master, which I'm sure she did on a regular basis.

Byron turned slightly and gestured to Anastasia, who moved swiftly to his side.

"Anastasia, my sweet Greek melon, will you be so kind as to continue the tour for our visitors?"

Addressing us, he said, "I am close to completing the third canto of my poem and eager to return to it." With that he left us with Anastasia.

Even though it was midday, the house was dark, as I've mentioned, due to the leaden skies. Anastasia carried a magnificently styled candle lamp with a glass shade, which looked like it may have come from the Court of Louis XVI. She stepped forward to lead the way up the staircase. The candlelight flashed on her silver bracelet, a heavy and well crafted ornament, with the patina of ancient Greece.

The bracelet caught Percy's eye. He was much more traveled than I, and had some knowledge of Grecian antiquities. "My God, that bracelet, where did you find it? It's the image of the Heracles knot masterpieces I've seen in the Athens Historical Museum, made popular in the second and third century."

He moved to her side to examine the bracelet more closely. "This is truly remarkable craftsmanship. Is it a family heirloom?"

Anastasia raised her arm, studying the bangle on her arm as if she hadn't seen it before. She set her lamp on the first step of the stairway and slipped the bracelet from her wrist. "It is but a poor copy, I think." She extended her hand towards Percy. "You can have it if you wish."

Percy's eyes widened, and he remained silent for a moment before shaking his head. "No, I really couldn't accept it. If this is genuine it would be a price-less treasure. How did you come by it? Was it a gift from Lord Byron?"

She offered a sly smile. "Not at all. I found it in a small village so many years ago I've forgotten the name of the place."

I thought then it was a curious thing to say from someone so young, but I assumed she was making a small joke.

She collected her lamp, and moved toward the staircase, saying, "Please watch your step."

Upstairs we were introduced to the dining room where we would spend the next three nights in conversation, drinking wine and eventually reading ghost stories.

"The house was built in 1710 by its original owner Giovanni Diodati," she informed us in a slow cadence, as though she thought we might not under-stand her accented English. "Professor Diodati was born in Geneva, but his family was Italian."

We were inside one of the large bedrooms at the end of the hall where a portrait of a dour man in robes was displayed. "This is the Professor," she said, pointing to the portrait.

Claire, who had taken an instant dislike to Anastasia, spoke up in her most imperious tone; "You refer to him as 'Professor.' He looks to me to be nothing more than a common parish minister."

Anastasia turned from the portrait, the flickering light from the lamp she carried accenting her high cheekbones and flawless olive skin. She stared at Claire for an uncomfortably long time, inclining her head in that peculiar way I mentioned, not saying a word. Anastasia finally spoke. "He was only twenty-one when he was named professor of Hebrew at the Genevan Academy, and in 1608 became professor of theology."

Flustered, Claire replied with a hint of sarcasm in her voice, "Oh, is that all?"

"Not quite," Anastasia said. "The Professor also is known for translating the Bible into Italian in 1603."

I stood amazed at the breadth of her knowledge, and assumed she'd been educated in Switzerland, which turned out not to be the case.

She continued staring at Claire, perhaps anticipating another question. When none came, she opened the doors leading onto a balustrade balcony surrounding three sides of the house. A damp wind blew off the lake, and I crossed my arms over my breasts to warm myself.

Villa Diodati was perched upon a small hill with an impressive view of Lake Geneva and the Jura Mountains in the distance. That day the heavily overcast skies obscured the snow-capped mountains.

"It is a shame we're unable to enjoy the beauty of this view," Percy said, adding, "The lake is one of the largest in Switzerland, is it not?"

Anastasia turned her gaze on Percy. "Lac Léman, as the locals call it, is by far the largest and deepest body of water in Switzerland, and one of the largest in Western Europe."

She paused, studying us, and I noticed for the first time how her dark eyes held the meager light from her lamp and cast it back like the a beacon in the night.

"While much of the geography surrounding the Alps dates back to man's prehistory, the formation of these lakes is fairly recent, perhaps only ten thousand years ago, created by a retreating glacier."

Almost in unison, Claire, Percy, and I turned from looking out at the crescent shaped lake to gape at this servant girl who had uttered what was one of the wildest fabrications I'd ever heard in my eighteen years. I could only shake my head at her audaciousness. We looked at one another for a moment.

Claire snorted. Percy coughed and smiled politely.

Anastasia merely pointed to the open doors, the exquisite bracelet sliding along her wrist, and led us silently through the bedroom Percy and I would occupy for the next few nights, and back down the stairs.

Chapter Two

Later that evening, I found myself alone with Dr. Polidori in the library, where I had gone to fetch a book after dinner. A rainstorm of some consequence had drummed incessantly all evening, and Lord Byron had insisted we spend the night rather than return to our cottage.

We all agreed since no one wished to chance becoming a target for the frequent lightning strikes illuminating the night sky. Also we had consumed numerous bottles of an excellent Bordeaux at dinner.

For some reason, Polidori had become infatuated with me, and he tried to make his intentions known, as men are wont to do. He sidled next to me as I reached for a book.

"You are truly a lovely young woman, Madame Shelley," he said in hushed tones. "I understand that you and Mr. Shelley are not yet married?"

This was indeed a true statement. At the time Percy was still legally married to Harriet, his first wife and mother of his child. Though not yet wedded, I'd taken to calling myself Mrs. Shelley. Poor Harriet committed suicide later that year, and Percy and I married soon after.

None of this was Dr. Polidori's business, however, but I did not wish to be rude. Besides, he was a most attractive man, and I was feeling more than a bit tipsy. "We're as good as husband and wife," I said. "We're of one mind on that."

We were alone in the library except for one of the cats prowling through the stack, but Dr. Polidori leaned in towards me as if about to share a secret he wished only the two of us to hear. His hip pressed against my own.

"Are you saying only the poet is able to lay his head upon your beautiful breasts? What about a lovesick doctor?"

I'd like to say I was shocked since Dr. Polidori and I were barely acquainted, but I fancied myself a modern woman in those days, naive as that may sound. My circle of friends included poets, writers, and artists who believed the new century would bring huge advancements in science, and the puritanical moral strictures would be cast aside.

Percy and I had defied the conventions of our day, so I was not offended by Polidori's forthright solicitations. To be perfectly honest, I felt drawn to the handsome doctor, and more than a little flattered by his advances. But I wasn't about to give in to my baser self. Not yet, anyway.

I quickly changed the subject. "What do you know of Lord Byron's servant girl? The Greek one."

"Ah, you mean Anastasia. I'm afraid she's already spoken for. She is George's favorite of the moment."

"Do you find her odd?" I asked.

"In what way?"

I told him about her explanation of the formation of the lake. "She said this with the greatest authority, and expected us to believe her. We all knew it was wild speculation, and I felt embarrassed for the girl."

"Actually, what she said makes a good deal of sense, though it's been some time since I studied the geologic sciences. I'm sure it was simply conjecture on her part."

"What is her background? Where did she attend school?"

Polidori shook his head. "As far as I know she has no formal education. George found her working as a hotel maid on one of his trips across Italy and hired her on the spot. He seems mightily attached to her."

By this time, I had selected a book and said, "We should return to the others or they may get the wrong impression." I ran a fingertip along his patrician nose, and lowered my eyes demurely.

We rejoined the others in the dining room where Byron and Percy were in a heated discussion about the meaning of Luigi Galvani's experiments with dead frogs. Claire was seated near the fire, snoring softly. Anastasia stood nearby holding a decanter of wine, listening to the conversation, her head tilted in that peculiar way.

"Don't you see what it means?" Byron was saying. "If we can animate a dead frog, then all things are possible. Who is to say we can't do the same with humans?"

Percy seemed to be of two minds on the subject. "Agreed, Dr. Galvani has moved science in a new direction with his discovery of animal electricity, but animating a man is completely different than a frog's leg."

Byron shook his head stubbornly. "We've entered a new era where each day science tears down another brick in the wall of ignorance. Anything is possible, even bringing people back from the dead."

The thought chilled me, but I hung on each word while they debated the subject for more than an hour. Polidori injected a level-headedness to the discussion, using his medical experience to explain the difference between making a frog's leg twitch, and bringing it back to life.

They went on in that fashion until Byron yawned loudly. He swallowed the last of his wine, and wiped his mouth with the back of his hand. Anastasia was there in a flash to refill the crystal goblet, but Byron stayed her hand. He gazed at Anastasia admiringly, stroked her arm, and said, "Thank you, my dear, but I've had enough wine and conversation for one night. You may prepare my bed now." He gave her a familiar tap to the backside and sent her on her way.

To us, he said, "We should continue this discussion tomorrow over dinner." He excused himself and followed Anastasia to his bedchamber.

***

I awoke in the middle of the night from an alarming dream in which a faceless man was chasing me. I ran for my life, but he cut the distance as though I stood motionless. He drew closer, and I saw he was only part human. Some of his appendages seemed to have been torn from the bodies of other species. Blood dripped from mangled arms and legs protruding from his hideous frame.

The dream distressed me deeply, and I was unable to return to my slumber. I climbed from the high poster bed, bundled myself in a blanket, and walked into the hall. Our chamber was the very same room we'd visited earlier, the one containing Professor Diodati's portrait. Claire's chamber was at the other end of the hall, while Byron's and Polidori's rooms were downstairs, with most of the servants staying in the carriage house behind the manor.

The rain had subsided by then, and I heard the haunting cry of the peacock calling out for a mate, perhaps. I strode to the balcony overlooking the first floor to see if I could spot the lovesick fowl, instead spying a shadowed figure tiptoeing from Lord Byron's bedchamber. At first I assumed the nocturnal visitor was Byron's lover, Anastasia, but when she passed one of the candelabras situated near the bottom of the stairwell, it became clear it was none other than my half-sister Claire.

I slid behind a column, and hid there until Claire entered her chamber and closed the door. It appeared as though Claire's wishes had come true, and she was back in Byron's affections, or at least back in his bed. Everyone knew Lord Byron's affections were famously short lived.

As though to prove my point, I heard more footsteps from below. I peered over the balcony in time to see another figure cross the hall and enter Byron's room. The comings and goings reminded me of the traffic in Trafalgar Square, and I had to bite my lip to keep from laughing aloud. This person wasn't difficult to identify as she carried the same lamp as when she gave us a tour of the manor earlier that afternoon.

It was Anastasia. I had to marvel at her daring, and Lord Byron's stamina.

That same morning, Percy awoke to find me stroking his chest beneath his bedclothes. After imagining the amorous adventures transpiring in Byron's bedchamber that night, I felt sexually charged and wanting—no, needing—physical intimacy. I knew Percy would be more than happy to oblige me.

And indeed Percy rose to the occasion.

We were soon making loud and passionate love. In the midst of it, I happened to glance toward the chamber door, and realized I had left it partly open after my earlier perambulations. Neither the door nor whether we would wake anyone with our energetic coupling was uppermost on my mind at the moment, but I chanced to see Anastasia scrutinizing us through the open door. Her head was cocked, and she seemed to be appraising us as if she was unfamiliar with the act of coitus, though from what I'd heard and seen that was far from the case.

Instead of being shocked by her intrusion into our lovemaking, I became further aroused and attacked Percy with abandon. We completed our act, climaxing together and falling apart in a state of blissful exhaustion. My breathing eventually returned to normal, and I was surprised to see Anastasia still observing us. I nudged Percy and pointed to our voyeur.

"Anastasia, if you would care for a closer view, why don't you join us here in bed?" Percy laughed as he said this, and patted the mattress.

She may have thought he was joking, but knowing Percy as I did, I assumed he hoped she would take him up on his offer. Anastasia said nothing. She backed away, closing the door behind her.

Much later, I went to the kitchen to brew us a pot of tea while Percy stayed abed recovering from our bout of lovemaking. From the kitchen I heard Byron's voice talking to someone about my half-sister Claire. Curious, I moved to the doorway and saw Byron and Polidori at the dining room table. Neither could see me, so I lingered there listening to the conversation.

"I have no real feelings for her," Byron was saying, "but a man is a man, and if a girl of eighteen comes prancing to me in the middle of the night, there is but one thing to do."

Both men laughed. "Quite a predicament, you have, Lord Byron."

"Yes," Byron agreed. "She is so very needy for my touch I almost feel sorry for her. At least the dalliance with Claire gave me some reprieve from the Greek girl."

"Anastasia?"

"That woman wears me out. She can go on and on for hours without tiring. She even came to me after Claire had departed last night. I could barely walk from my chamber this morning."

They laughed again, and I retreated to the kitchen to pour the tea. I felt disheartened for poor Claire, though she surely knew what sort of man Byron was after he abandoned her. Some women will always lead with their hearts, no matter how many times they are burned.

Before I could return to our chamber with the tea, Anastasia entered the kitchen. I took the opportunity to question her about her voyeuristic behavior.

"Anastasia, about last night. I'm curious as to why you intruded on such a private moment."

She regarded me for a full minute in that strange way of hers before responding, "Watching and learning, Madame Shelley. Watching and learning. That seems to be my mission in life."

She then apologized for her offense, and returned to her work.

Later, I told Percy of our brief conversation in the kitchen, and Anastasia's unexpected statement. He smiled, and said, "She must have wanted to watch a real woman make love. Now she can please George even more."

"From what I heard, Anastasia needs no such lessons."

He looked at me with great anticipation, but I decided to keep him in the dark regarding Byron's opinion of her sexual fortitude.

Chapter Three

After dinner that evening we all gathered around the fireplace. Outside, lightning flashed and barrages of thunder shook the manor. During dinner, Percy and Byron had talked incessantly about their future writing projects. That conversation waned as we settled into comfortable chairs and pulled the lamps close in an attempt to drive away the gloom.

We had all consumed copious amounts of wine through dinner, and as we sat around a low polished table made of some exotic wood, Anastasia brought us a full decanter of red wine along with clean goblets. Byron surprised us by emptying a vial of a reddish-brown liquid into the wine and stirring it.

"Laudanum," he said before I could ask. "I find it stimulates the imagination, and helps me with my writing."

I had heard of laudanum, of course, as the tincture of opium was credited with great medicinal powers, but I'd never had occasion to sample it. I was more than willing to continue the festive mood, but if I'd known how dramatically the atmosphere would change, I might have reconsidered my actions.

By this time, everyone had taken note of Polidori's amorous attentions to my person, especially Percy, who had nearly come to blows with the physician that afternoon. Tensions were high, and all of us drank of the fortified wine far more than necessary.

After one concussive blast of thunder, Byron exclaimed, "The night is perfect for ghost stories." He had with him a copy of *Fantasmagoriana*, a collection of German ghost stories. Byron insisted we take turns reading from the anthology, which only added to the claustrophobic atmosphere.

I read from Heinrich Clauren's fantastical story, *The Grey Room*, and Byron from Laun's *The Death Bride*, which caused Percy to shiver and pour the remainder of the wine into his glass. He downed it in one long swallow. Anastasia was there within seconds to replace the decanter.

We heard a shutter flapping from one of the bedchamber windows. I felt a cold gust of wind blow through the drafty house, guttering the candles, and casting sinister shadows upon the walls. The odor of smoke hung in the air along with the aura of dread created by the ghost stories.

A frosty shudder advanced from the nape of my neck down my back. I pulled my shawl tighter around my bare shoulders. Polidori shed his jacket and wrapped it around me with a flourish.

"A lovely woman shouldn't suffer from this intemperate weather," he said, squeezing my shoulder affectionately.

Percy started to rise from his chair, his fists balled, but I shook my head and he settled shakily into his seat. It was clear the wine and laudanum had had its effect on my sweet Percy. I could see he was teetering on the ledge of rationality, swaying between belligerent paranoia and unconsciousness.

Byron broke the tension by suggesting we should write our own ghost stories. There ensued some spirited conversation between Polidori and Byron, with Percy coming awake enough to add a few thoughts of his own. I listened as the men talked of long dead spirits molesting unsuspecting maidens. Of human hearts transferred into the bodies of wild primates. Of animals able to change their appearance at will. Of ancient beings surviving on the lifeblood of humans.

Both Byron and Polidori were excited about this last gruesome idea of blood-sucking creatures, but it sent another chill tramping across my back.

Claire had retired to her chambers long before, but I found the discussion fascinating. Anastasia must have also since she had crept closer to the table, and now stood with one hand on the back of Byron's chair, listening with rapt attention. They bantered back and forth, each proposing a chilling premise for their stories. I was left with nagging doubts about whether I could contribute anything worthwhile after listening to the intriguing speculations of these creative minds.

I saw that Percy was nearly asleep, and nudged him. "We should excuse ourselves," I suggested.

"But not before hearing Coleridge's latest," Byron insisted. "I was able to purchase one of the first published copies of his epic poem, *Christabel*."

"I've heard it's his master work," Polidori said. "Read it to us, George. You have just the voice for it."

Percy came awake, as I knew he greatly respected Coleridge, and had many times praised *The Rime of the Ancient Mariner.*

Byron began reading the poem, affecting the tone and dramatic intensity of a Shakespearean stage actor. Considering the turbulent weather with the lightning and thunder rolling off the mountains and across the lake, and the intoxicating effects of the stimulants we'd ingested, Byron's recitation had the effect of unnerving us all.

The shadowed walls seemed to press in on me. I felt a throbbing in my chest, and the taste of bile on my tongue. I had no idea how Byron's reading was affecting the others until he read this passage from the poem:

Like one that shuddered, she unbound
The cincture from beneath her breast:
Her silken robe, and inner vest,
Dropt to her feet, and in full view,
Behold! her bosom and half her side—

Percy's eyes suddenly went wide. He threw up his hands with an eerie scream and dashed from the room, his chair crashing to the floor behind him.

Byron paused momentarily, glancing at me, and then to Percy's fleeing figure.

He shrugged and smiled apologetically.

"I didn't think your recitation was that bad," Polidori said to Byron.

I leaped from my chair, dropping Polidori's coat to the floor, and chased after Percy. Behind me I heard Byron's voice as he commenced reading once again.

I found Percy lying on our bed, a down pillow covering his head. I removed the pillow and asked, "What gave you such a fright?"

He sat up and covered my cheek with wet kisses. "I'm so sorry, but I had the most terrible vision." His hands were trembling.

I couldn't imagine what he saw, but felt it must have been instigated by the wine and laudanum he'd consumed. "Perhaps it would help if you share your vision with me."

He seemed hesitant to tell me, his eyes darting from my face to my bosoms.

"Please tell me," I insisted.

"Promise you won't think me insane."

I promised, and he said, "As Byron read that last passage of the woman dropping her robe to the floor, I saw you in the same state of undress, but ..."

"But what?"

"Your breasts were bare, but instead of nipples, there were eyes staring back at me." His face had turned ashen as he spoke.

He may have been shocked by the vision, but it struck me as humorous. To calm him, I said, "I can assure you there are no eyes on my breasts, except those of your own when you look upon me."

He placed a hand on my bosoms. "How can I be sure? You'll have to show me."

And so I did.

Chapter Four

I awoke late the next morning to find the storm had cleared some of the clouds away, and patches of blue peered through the overcast sky. Lying there, my thoughts returned to the ghost story we were to write and deliver to the group that evening. A number of fanciful ideas came to me as I lay abed listening to Percy snore, but none of them felt compelling enough to capture anyone's attention. It was time, I decided, to become serious about the project.

Villa Diodati contained a lovely courtyard that had remained unoccupied these last few days due to the inclement weather. Even though the temperature was still brisk, I was determined to sit outside to work on my story. I threw a blanket around my shoulders, and collected my journal, pen and ink well.

On the way to the courtyard Anastasia stopped me to ask if I wished to have breakfast. I told her I was going to sit in the courtyard to work on my story. She offered to bring me croissants and a pot of tea, which I gratefully accepted.

Sitting outside, I struggled to coerce an original idea from my still besotted brain. Most of what I'd heard discussed the night before were variations on the themes of the German stories we'd read. I wished to find something original, not derivative of another's work. I took pen in hand and wrote of a woman who dreams of a monstrous beast with glowing red eyes and coils of snakes wrapped around its body. She awakens to find the beast has come to life and it devours her.

Anastasia brought the tea and croissants to my table as I was writing.

"What is your story about?" she asked.

I told her my idea of the snake-giant and the woman. She remained silent, but I felt she was not overly impressed with my fiction. "What do you think?"

She didn't answer immediately, but was obviously deliberating her reply. She fingered the silver bracelet while looking down at my journal. She shrugged, and said, "Not a bad subject for a ghost story, but the original is much more frightening."

"The original?"

"In Greek mythology, no monster was more feared by the gods than Typhon. He was described as a giant, so tall his head touched the stars, and while he had the head and torso of a man, they were wrapped by coils of snakes, hissing and writhing menacingly."

I thought about that and wondered if I'd previously read about this Typhon monster and somehow pulled it from my subconscious. "I suspect there are many monsters to be found in mythology," I said.

"To be sure," Anastasia replied. "Some of mankind's earliest writings can be found on the stone tablets of Mesopotamia where men wrote stories of heroes journeying to netherworlds, fighting demons, and vanquishing monsters."

By this time nothing Anastasia said surprised me. Her head seemed to be filled with a wealth of arcane knowledge from across the ages. "Then maybe I should use one of these ancient myths as the basis for a contemporary story."

She sat down in the chair opposite me, and poured tea into the cup she'd brought. I took it and inhaled the warm fragrance. "So what do you think?"

This time she didn't hesitate. "If I were to write a story, even a ghost story, I'd want it to touch on the human condition, the universal elements affecting all men. Fear of the unknown is one circumstance you can exploit, but what we fear most of all is something we live with every day."

"And what is that?"

"Death, Madame Shelley, death. Human beings have great potential, but they're constrained by a grotesquely short life span. Think about it. Compared to other organisms, your life is over in the blink of an eye. Some trees live for thousands of years. Even the lowly sponge has been known to survive deep below the sea for fifty or more human generations."

"You're saying I should write about our short life spans?"

"Not directly, but about how to either extend it or …" She paused and cocked her head, her eyes closed as though listening to an internal voice.

"Or what?" I prompted.

"Or perhaps how to bring people back to life after they've died."

"Now you sound like Byron and Dr. Polidori," I said, remembering their conversation from two nights ago about Galvani's experiments with the frog legs. "Besides, bringing people back from the dead isn't original either. Jesus brought Lazarus to life—at least the Bible declares it so—though every educated person knows the Bible is nothing more than fables and morality tales."

She considered my words, nodding slightly. The sun had broken through the clouds, and diamonds of light danced across her dark eyes. "Jesus commanded his apostles to 'Heal the sick, raise the dead, cleanse the lepers, and cast out devils.' And Peter raised Tabitha from the dead, and St. Paul raised Eutychus."

"Stories told to children and the simple-minded."

"Believe what you wish, but imagine the possibilities if we could bring life to the dead."

She said it with such conviction that I began to think of my own life, and the people I'd lost. I thought about the mother I never knew, of my own daughter, dead within days of leaving my womb. Would I bring them back to life if I could? Deep in my soul I knew I would do all in my power to make it so.

"But how would such a thing be possible?"

"It may not be possible, not in your lifetime, but think of the potential of electricity."

"You mean like Galvani's experiment animating the frog leg?"

"Yes, but on a much larger scale. The power to animate a human body would have to come from a force much stronger than a static charge. Perhaps from a lightning bolt."

Excited by the idea, I scribbled fiercely in my journal. When I looked up, Anastasia was gone, and Percy was wending his way shakily toward the table.

I was reluctant to tell Percy about our conversation, or Anastasia's suggestion for a story. The tale hung by a single delicate thread. It lacked the underpinnings of plot, purpose, and character.

Percy helped me eat the croissants and finish the tea. By then, he seemed refreshed, but I felt seized by a deep lethargy. I knew the night's story telling would go late into morning, and I needed to rest.

I excused myself, saying, "If I don't nap, I'll not stay awake for tonight's debauchery."

"We can't have that, can we?" He kissed me on the mouth in parting, saying he would find Byron, and maybe they would go sailing if the weather permitted.

Back in the warmth of our bed, I fell quickly asleep, though I found my repose fitful, filled with macabre dreams. One of the dreams was a manifestation so dark and frightful that I woke with a start. As I lay clutching the heavy comforter, the nightmarish actions of the dream came alive once again, and I realized this was the genesis of my story. I later documented the dream in my journal, writing,

I saw the pale student of unhallowed arts kneeling beside the thing he had put together. I saw the hideous phantasm of a man stretched out, and then, on the working of some powerful engine, show signs of life and stir with an uneasy, half vital motion. Frightful must it be; for supremely frightful would be the effect of any human endeavor to mock the stupendous mechanism of the Creator of the world.

That evening I related the central thread of my story. The men seemed surprised by the concept, probably not believing I could create such a ghastly premise by myself. They encouraged me to complete it, and Percy later insisted I expand the ghost story into a novel.

We left Lake Geneva and Villa Diodati behind not long after that night of

story telling, but I thought often about the strange Greek girl, and her com-
manding presence. I am convinced she helped me breathe life into my story of
a monster created from the scraps of corpses.

***

Two years later, the fragment of a story that grew from a bad dream I had
on the shores of Lake Geneva was finally published. I titled the book, *Frankenstein: or, The Modern Prometheus*, and was surprised by the acceptance it received
from the reading public.

I decided I should thank Anastasia for her assistance, and thought I'd send
her a gift of a few pounds, along with a signed copy of the book. Since Percy
remained good friends with Lord Byron, I asked if he would inquire if Anastasia was still in his employ.

Months went by, and I'd all but forgotten my request when Percy entered
the study of our apartment one afternoon holding a sheaf of papers.

"She's gone," he said.

"Who's gone?" I had no idea who he was talking about.

"Anastasia. This is a letter from George, in answer to my query about her
whereabouts. He said Anastasia returned to her home in Greece shortly after
we departed Switzerland. He tried to find her, hoping to entice her to return
to his service, but no one knew where she went. He said there had been an
influenza outbreak in the region and he feared she may have succumbed."

I was heartsick. "Poor Anastasia. She was such a remarkable individual,
striking in so many ways, don't you think?"

Percy agreed and we fondly recalled our holiday on Lake Geneva during
the summer that was no summer.

Chapter Five

And now, dear reader, I move on to the saddest of days, which will move my story to its final chapter. Unfortunately, the beginning of the end starts with another death. The love of my life perished in July of 1822. Always enamored with the sea, it seemed fitting Percy should die in its embrace, but why at such a young age, leaving me alone to raise our son, Percy Florence?

His schooner was caught in a violent summer storm and foundered while returning from a visit with Lord Byron and his friend Leigh Hunt at Livorno, Italy. Poor Percy's body washed ashore several days later, and he was cremated right there on the beach. Byron and Hunt were in attendance in my stead.

They told me his heart refused to burn, and so they delivered it to me. I still hold it among my most precious possessions. Percy's remains were buried in the Protestant Cemetery in Rome, and several years later I had occasion to visit Italy with young Percy Florence. Naturally, I wished to see Percy's final resting place, and show little Percy where his father was buried.

On that warm August afternoon, I bought a bouquet of flowers from a street vendor, and we made our way to the cemetery. We found his grave near an ancient pyramid in the city walls. His gravestone bore the Latin inscription, *Cor Cordium*, "Heart of Hearts," and below that, in reference to his death at sea, were these lines from Shakespeare's *The Tempest*:

'Nothing of him that doth fade
But doth suffer a sea-change
Into something rich and strange'

"He was a man of immense talents," I told my son after we had placed the flowers at the head of the grave.

"You miss him greatly, do you not, Mother?"

I stood quietly with my head bowed for a minute before answering. I felt tears pooling in my eyes and commence streaming down my cheeks. Sniffling, I held my son close, whispering in his ear, "Oh, so much more than you can imagine, sweet child. But I have you to remind me of our love for one another."

We stood together in silence until something caught my eye on the edge of the grave, half-hidden in the shadows cast by a towering cedar. It was a small, neatly wrapped package, the paper nearly the same color as the white marble stone. Before I could retrieve it, however, I heard a movement behind me. I turned to see a man of middle age, dressed in the clothing of an English gentleman, with long waistcoat and high silk hat.

He was leaning against the city wall only ten feet from where we stood. He was a mostly unremarkable man, and I was certain I'd never seen him before, but there was something familiar that compelled me to approach him.

As I neared, I could see he was studying me intently, his head cocked at a curious angle. A slight smile played over his lips, and his dark eyes were alight with an internal glow that belied the shadows surrounding him.

"Excuse me, sir, but do I know you?"

He didn't reply.

"Did you know my husband?"

"You might say I was one of his many admirers." His voice was steady, but I found the tone to be slightly mocking, almost arrogant.

"What are you doing here?" A hint of anger edged my voice.

He gave me another bout of exasperating silence, taking his time digesting my question as if deciding whether to swallow or spit out an answer.

"Watching and learning, Madame Shelley. Watching and learning. That seems to be my mission in life."

I believe my mouth may have fallen open upon hearing his rejoinder. He touched the brim of his top hat and walked away, disappearing through a gate in the city walls.

As I write this now, I must assume you are as shocked by this turn of events as I was. My mind churned as we made our way back to the hotel, turning the matter one way and the other, but never finding a satisfying answer to the enigma. How could it be, I asked myself over and over, that some ten years after Anastasia disappeared, presumably dead, a man nearly twice her age appears with the same mannerisms, reciting the exact same phrase she once did?

It made as much sense to me as if I'd heard Percy's voice hailing me from beneath his gravestone. The matter troubled me throughout our European holiday.

***

Back in London later that year, I was invited to a literary gathering to honor the poet Elizabeth Barrett Browning. Among the guests was the scholar Hugh Stuart Boyd. Mr. Boyd was an Englishman, and though blind when I met him, he was still considered one of the most brilliant men of his generation. I'd heard he'd been teaching Greek to Ms. Browning, a kindly woman who had sent me a condolence note after Percy's death.

When speaking with Mr. Boyd that evening, he inquired about the events leading to my writing of the Frankenstein novel. The story of our evenings at Byron's Villa Diodati had spread, growing to scandalous proportions as gossipers added their own salacious, and mostly fictitious, details.

It wasn't the first time I'd been asked about those nights in Lake Geneva, and it wouldn't be the last, but I was eager to set the record straight for Mr. Boyd. I told him about the ghost stories we'd read, and how Lord Byron had challenged us to write our own story. And because Mr. Boyd was a Greek scholar, I mentioned Anastasia's role, and described her amazing knowledge of world history.

He was fascinated by my tale, especially after I told him of the man in the cemetery. He chortled, saying, "Then she has surely lived up to her name."

"Why is that?"

"In the Greek language, Anastasia means, 'One who is reborn,' so your mystery cemetery caller must have been Anastasia paying you another visit."

He laughed heartily at the apparent absurdity of such a thing, and I feigned to join him for I already knew the truth of the matter.

***

I sit here today, in the winter of 1851, pen in shaky hand, writing on the last page of what may be the final journal I ever complete. Percy Florence is a grown man. It has been over twenty years since the two of us visited the cemetery in Rome and chanced upon the man in the top hat. The man's words, though, still ring in my ears—

Watching and learning. That seems to be my mission in life.

I can close my eyes and hear the words, picturing not the man's face, but Anastasia as she stood in the kitchen of Villa Diodati that blustery day in 1816. I hear her expound upon Lake Geneva's glacial formation some ten thousand years before. I can see her peering through the doorway into our bedchamber observing Percy and I making love. And I can still hear her voice as we discussed the possibility of bringing the dead to life.

As I write this final chapter, I leave it to you to determine the truth of what you've read here. Was I a participant in a supernatural event, or was it only a riddle of my own making? Before you rush to judgment and assign it all to the bewildered ravings of an infirm woman, let me take you back to the encounter at Percy's gravesite. After hearing the man in the top hat echo those words I'd heard a decade before, I retreated in a state of shock, completely forgetting about the packet I'd spied moments earlier. Unbeknownst to me, my son had retrieved it and slipped it into my coat pocket.

My mind was awhirl with turbulent thoughts. I barely remember walking back to the hotel, and it wasn't until much later that I discovered the small box in my coat pocket, hidden in the folds of a scarf.

Would that Percy had been there when I unwrapped the package and opened the box. He was such a lover of all things mystical and fantastical, he would have cut right to the heart of this queer episode. For you see, what was in that box is the key to this entire drama. It once hung on Anastasia's slender wrist. Now the silver Heracles knot bracelet Percy so admired dangles heavily from my wrist, even as I write these words.

My experiences with Anastasia have taught me all things are possible. I'd like to believe this ancient Greek bracelet contains the power of resurrection. Or perhaps, you might say, my story is no more than the maundering of a mind blighted by death, braced by copious amounts of laudanum, which I consume regularly to help me through bouts of melancholia and failing health.

You can believe what you wish, but for me the choice is a simple one. I choose to believe the bracelet is an offering from beyond the grave, a magical connection to those days we spent in Villa Diodati when a servant girl named Anastasia helped me bring a monster back from the dead, and also opened my eyes to the mysteries of life.

Does the bracelet hold the power to reverse the natural order of things? Like Anastasia's name, will I be reborn if I'm still wearing it after my heart stops beating? Ah, that is the last great question, is it not, and I sense the answer will soon become apparent. My story will either come to an abrupt end, or if perchance Anastasia has passed along the gift of renewal, then there may be more journals to write.

Until the moment of enlightenment, all I can do is watch and learn. That is my final mission in life.

THE FINAL WHISPER

About ten years ago I noticed a swooshing noise in my left ear. The swoosh cycled constantly, pitched at a frequency that might not shatter crystal, but threatened to shred my sanity. It seemed to pulse with my heartbeat, droning on morning and night. Not content to bombard me on one side, the noise soon spread to my right ear.

The noise is always with me. Sometimes, other, louder sounds like music playing on the radio, the blaring of the TV, or even one-on-one conversations will cause the noise to fade into the background. But in the quiet of my office while trying to concentrate on my writing, or lying in bed at night, the phantom noise in my head is more than distracting. It can be insufferable.

As I soon learned, I had joined the millions of men and women afflicted with tinnitus, the false perception of sound in the absence of acoustic stimuli. Tinnitus is a common clinical syndrome affecting twelve percent of men and almost fourteen percent of women who are sixty-five and older. More shocking, tinnitus affects nearly half of all soldiers who were exposed to blasts in Iraq and Afghanistan.

To a writer, any subject can be grist for the story mill, including phantom noises that can be as piercing as a dentist's drill, or as cringe inducing as nails on a chalkboard. Who might suffer the most from this internal plague, I asked myself, which in some people has triggered thoughts of suicide. It seemed to me that a musician who found his life upended by a particularly virulent form of tinnitus was the perfect character for my budding story.

And so "Mad Max" Gribbins was born. The former lead guitarist for a popular rock band, The Kingslayers, Max is forced to quit the band because of his tinnitus. The story soon took on a life of its own as Max's tinnitus evolved into something he would never have expected. The cacophony of noise that had plagued Max for so many years is replaced by ghostly whispers, which become oh, so much more.

I have personal experience with tinnitus, but this new phenomenon that Max was dealing with was beyond the range of anyone's understanding. I wasn't sure how Max would deal with the new noises in his head, and to be honest with you, I didn't know where the ghostly whispers were taking me. The saga of Max Gribbins continued to grow until it was more than a short story. In fact, it's about a third the size of a full-length novel at nearly 100 pages.

Read on and you'll learn how Max copes with his problems and why he says he has a Tin Man in his head.

ghostly
whispers

Ghostly Whispers

CHAPTER ONE
The Tin Man

Max Gribbins told everyone he had a Tin Man living inside his head. A Tin Man with a horn. Everyone laughed, thinking it was all a joke. He even managed to get a smile out of Wanda Sue, who was probably delighted, thinking his tinnitus condition had accelerated to the point he was becoming delusional.

After his first visit to the ENT specialist he learned there was no cure for tinnitus. He would have to live with the constant ringing in his ears for the rest of his life. Over the years the ringing had escalated from a distracting nuisance into a clamoring cascade that scrambled his thoughts and pushed him into sullen silences.

It was like a stranger had moved into his head. Uninvited. And packing an assortment of vuvuzelas, the South African plastic horns blown incessantly during the World Cup Games. Sometimes the noise became so overwhelming Max felt sure the Tin Man had cloned himself and was now a quartet, or at least a trio. He could picture the Tin Man Group taking positions behind his eardrums, maybe standing on their tiptoes stretching to hit the high notes. Sharing high fives with each piercing blast.

Max recognized the looks of doubt—and sometimes pity—he always got when he tried to explain how the noises were driving him over a crumbling ledge of sanity. They probably thought his years of living in a chemical-induced fog had pickled his brain and he had lapsed into a paranoid fantasy world. But the Tin Man was no fantasy. He was there every second of his life, and he was getting more brazen. Blowing his insane horns night and day, varying the pitch, volume and intensity just enough to keep him off balance.

Max decided drastic measures must be taken or he'd lose his mind. He knew Wanda Sue would tell him not to bother. She'd say he lost his freaking mind about the same time he quit his gig with The Kingslayers seven years ago. But she had no idea how his chronic tinnitus had changed his life. Nothing he'd tried screened out the tsunami of whistles and screeches battering his brain. And he'd tried everything. Vitamins. White noise machines. Exercise and diet. Each night he drank himself to sleep, but even when he passed out the noise woke him and he spent hours in the dark listening to the sounds pulsating in his head and the disgusting racket emanating from his bedmate.

Wanda Sue's snores sounded like a symphony by a deranged composer. The first movement, a slow and steady Sonata-Allegro tempo of nasal breaths, each one rising and falling in a wheezing intake of air. The second movement, the Scherzo, followed directly with a sloppy contrapuntal expulsion of air that sounded like she was making farting noises through her mouth. Wanda Sue's nocturnal symphonies continued until Max nudged her in the ribs with his elbow, and she'd roll over.

In search of relief, Max had even visited a meditation guru on the advice of Cappy, one of his former band mates. Cappy once studied with a Hindu master to help lick his longtime drug addiction. Using newly mastered relaxation and visioning techniques, Max imagined building a soundproof room around the Tin Man, boxing him in and exiling him to the far reaches of his head.

Lying awake with only Wanda Sue's snoring to keep him company, he began erecting the box, one wall at a time. He imagined a heavily insulated concrete slab ten inches thick. In his mind he used a miniature tractor and crane to haul the slabs and erect them. When the south wall went up, Max erected the other sides, then slowly, very slowly, slid the top and bottom slabs into place.

He envisioned a perfect box. A soundproof room. He pictured the Tin Man screaming in the dark of the room, claustrophobic fear freezing his vocal cords into silence. He could toot that damn horn of his all he wanted, but trapped inside the insulated prison of Max's mind not a squeak or buzz would be heard. At least that was how it was supposed to work, but the Tin Man wasn't playing his game. He laughed at his puny meditations. Doing his best impression of the big bad wolf, the Tin Man scoffed, *I'll huff and I'll puff and I'll blow your house down.*

And he did.

One of the doctors Max visited had suggested a daily regimen of exercise. He tried it for a while, joining a local gym and buying a treadmill, but after four months without any results, he abruptly quit. Now, aside from bending his elbow hefting glasses of scotch and beer, Max's only exercise was a forty-five minute daily walk through the small park near his house. Every afternoon, rain or shine, he'd walk briskly along the street bordering the park, cut across the playground and follow the half-mile nature trail to its end and back. He maintained the strict schedule not so much for health reasons, but to get away from Wanda Sue for at least part of the day.

Normally the natural sounds of the outdoors helped balance the riot in his head. But not on this day. Even with his iPod cranked to maximum volume, ear buds snuggled deep into his ears, the Tin Man blew so loud the maddening noise overshadowed the heavy rock music flowing from his iPod.

As he walked through the park that afternoon, Max Gribbins ignored the children on the playground swings, barely taking notice of the attractive young mothers chatting and laughing. In the past, he'd lucked out with a few of the women who thought a quick romp with a former rock star while the husband was at work was one of the benefits of suburban living. He didn't have time for any of that. Today, he told himself, he'd follow through with his plan. He'd been thinking about it for weeks, but lacked the nerve because, frankly, it was a completely insane idea. But true insanity was not doing anything, and the more he thought about it, the more resolute he became.

The idea had come to him one evening at dinner. He'd fallen into the habit of digging his forefinger into his left ear, rocking the fingertip back and forth as fast as he could. He did this so many times a day it had become an unconscious habit.

"For Christ's sake, will you take your finger out of your ear," Wanda Sue snarled at him. "You look like an inbred idiot. Next thing you'll be picking your nose at the table."

Max ignored her, his fingertip twitching faster and faster. Maybe it was his imagination, but for that few seconds the Tin Man seemed to fade away, his horn-tooting losing a little intensity. He eased his finger deeper into his ear canal, feeling the sharp edge of his nail scraping the tender membrane of his inner ear. The noise leeched through and around his finger, but he thought he was on to something. Maybe with the proper implement he might chase the infuriating trumpeter away for good.

Max knew he needed something firmer than his finger. Something stiff and smooth. He studied the fork and knife next to his plate, noting the sharp tines of the fork and inwardly wincing at the image of one of the tines puncturing his eardrum. He discounted the steak knife for the same reason, but after another sleepless night Max was game for anything.

The next morning Max sat at the kitchen counter with his third cup of coffee, his head throbbing more than usual. He'd swallowed two extra strength Advil's and was waiting for them to kick in. Trying to focus on anything but his massive headache and the accompanying rhythm section, Max stared blankly at the peach colored wall and the electrical wall plate next to the cabinet. Wanda Sue had decided on the color scheme and personally selected the furnishings and all the accessories in the house when they had it built. Standard wall plates weren't good enough for Wanda Sue, she wanted hand-rubbed antique bronze covers fringed with decorative filigrees. Each one cost Max nearly twenty dollars and there were fifty of the damn things around the house.

As he added the wall plates to the growing list of reasons to hate his wife, he noticed the two small screws sunk into the plate. There was nothing out of the ordinary about them, but the two Phillips head screws brought to mind an image of the screwdriver. Maybe what he needed was a little workshop therapy in the form of plunging a Phillips screwdriver into his ears? Would the tinnitus disappear? Would the Tin Man pack his bags and find a more hospitable host? Maybe he'd go completely deaf, but deafness couldn't be any worse than what he was living with now.

There was danger to such a procedure, of course. He might drive the tool entirely through his inner ear into his brain if he wasn't careful. He might end up a vegetable. Maybe dead. He didn't want that to happen. Or did he?

Resolutely, Max executed an abrupt about face and returned home.

"Hey, neighbor, how they hanging?" a cheery voice yelled out as he approached his house.

Tom Whitlow held a retractable leash in his hand. At the end of it two miniature schnauzers scampered toward Max, yapping playfully. Whitlow was freakishly tall, towering over his next-door neighbor and looking infinitely silly, Max thought, walking the two little dogs that reminded him of overgrown rats. Whitlow had pronounced laugh lines surrounding his eyes and mouth, but was otherwise good-looking in a way that the dark-skinned, pinch-faced Max Gribbins came to characterize as the "College Frat Boy Look."

Max knew some men of Whitlow's stature—he had to be at least 6'6"—were self conscious about their height. But that wasn't Tom Whitlow. No, Whitlow enjoyed lording it over his much shorter neighbor.

Whitlow and his wife Dana had bought the 3,500 square foot house two years ago in a short sale after the homeowners went underwater and moved out. His neighbor was a friendly, garrulous man who worked at home programming software for a major computer game company. When he wasn't walking the schnauzers, scattering dog crap through the neighborhood, or working on his computers, Whitlow was an ardent ham radio enthusiast. His neighbor had invited them over to see his set-up after they'd first moved to Valencia Park. Max didn't understand the appeal in sitting up half the night reaching out to other gasbags halfway around the world.

It all seemed so anachronistic, particularly in this day of email, Skype and Face Time. But Wanda Sue was fascinated and had returned often to visit with Tom and his radios. It occurred to Max that Wanda Sue and Whitlow might be communicating with each other in more intimate ways than radio waves, but he was thankful for every minute his wife left him alone.

"I see you're taking Zig and Zag on their daily crap walk," Max said as both dogs pawed at his legs.

He scuttled back a few steps, but Whitlow edged forward to follow him. His neighbor had an engaging smile, even white teeth in a broad, open face. His closely cropped blonde hair was tousled boyishly, and Max would bet if he looked at Tom Whitlow's third grade class picture he'd see the very same hairstyle.

Dana Whitlow worked for a company that supplied specialized computer systems to banks throughout the country, and she spent much of her time traveling to oversee the installation of the hardware. Max couldn't remember the last time she'd spent more than three consecutive days at home.

"You crack me up, Gribbins. I'll bet you were a riot on the concert circuit in your day. I'm sure they miss you, too. I hear they're playing the Garden next week as part of that big rock festival."

Fuck you and your two squirrely dogs. Whitlow liked to rub it in that Gribbins was no longer part of The Kingslayers, seemingly delighted to point out that the band was enjoying a resurgence of popularity since he left them.

"You're right, Tom. I've always been the life of the party." He turned away, walking swiftly toward the side entrance to his three-car garage.

"I'll catch ya later," Max said with a listless wave over his shoulder. "Got some work to do."

Inside the garage, Max made straight for the four-drawer tool cabinet tucked away in a corner behind the treadmill he'd bought after the doctor suggested exercise might help with his tinnitus. After he stopped using it, Wanda Sue tried the device for a week and never stepped on it again. She complained it made her sweat. Wanda Sue hated to sweat. Max could attest to that.

He shouldered past the treadmill to the red tool cabinet, noting the layer of dust blanketing the top. He rarely opened any of the drawers, and seldom used the expensive tools. When they'd built the house in the gated Florida community, he thought being a homeowner necessitated having tools to make repairs. He even considered taking up woodworking as a hobby. As the lead guitarist with The Kingslayers he'd proven he was good with his hands, so maybe he could build some of their furniture. Sure, and maybe Elvis was really alive and living in Costa Rica with Janis Joplin and John Lennon.

Max tugged open the top drawer of the cabinet, eying the huge pile of wrenches. There must be a hundred of them, he thought. Socket wrenches, ratchet wrenches, box end wrenches. All in standard and metric sizes. What the hell had he been thinking when he shelled out over a thousand bucks for a set of tools he never used?

Max shook his head, slid the drawer shut and opened the second drawer. He examined the stacks of screwdrivers, more than anyone would ever need in a lifetime of handyman work. He rooted through the maze of shafts, pulling out three or four of the Phillips screwdrivers before settling on one with a #2 stamped on the shank. The blade looked to be about four inches in length with a molded plastic grip. Max studied the tapered flutes of the Phillips' head, eyeing the blunt tip and pictured it sliding into his ear canal, slipping snugly against the Temporal bone and piercing the eardrum. He'd visited so many head doctors, stared at so many diagrams of the inner structure of the ear, he only needed to close his eyes to call up images of the malleus, and incus and semicircular canals.

Each doctor had given him the same diagnosis: tinnitus, nerve damage caused by his years of exposure to loud music. They showed him illustrations of the inner ear with its tiny hair cells acting as engineers to control the flow of sound from the auditory nerve to the brain. They explained that when these cells become damaged, bent or broken, they leak random electrical impulses to the brain.

He could only imagine the damage he'd done to his hair cells after years of playing with rock bands. His hair cells must look like a tornado swept through his canals. Whenever the ENT physicians explained about the hair cells and the electrical impulses they directed, he pictured a meadow of seagrass in a Disney cartoon, the plants alive, swaying and singing some insipid song while colorful carp swam in and out of the leaves of grass. But in his ears, voracious music-hating barracuda were devouring the grassy meadow and the clueless carp.

He hefted the screwdriver, feeling its satisfying weight. He slipped his fingers around the plastic grip and lifted it to his ear. The metal point felt cool and he let it sit on the edge of his outer ear for a moment, wondering if he had the courage to put a stop to the roaring. One sharp thrust would propel the point through the tympani membrane separating the outer ear from the middle and inner ear.

Max tightened his grip on the handle of the screwdriver. He gritted his teeth, closed his eyes and willed his hand to do the deed. The point pressed against his outer ear, and he winced in pain, jerking his head away from the tip of the tool.

"You're such a pussy," he muttered to himself.

He took a deep breath, closed his eyes again and envisioned bringing the Phillips up in one smooth motion and driving it into his right ear. For years, he'd used the same visioning technique before the band's concerts. Picturing his fingers flying over the strings with perfect licks. Playing memorable riffs, choreographing each move in his head.

He saw it clearly in his mind, and began his upward swing toward his ear, but the door from the house opened and Wanda Sue's grating voice echoed through the garage.

"Are you in here, Max?"

He dropped the screwdriver to his side, and turned to face her.

"What the hell are you doing over there with the toolbox?" The question was asked in the same tone of voice she'd used when she stepped in a smelly offering left in the front yard by one of Tom's schnauzers last week.

He sheepishly showed her the screwdriver. "I was going to tighten that loose screw on the pantry door." He thought it was a good spur-of-the-moment answer.

Wanda Sue stepped into the garage, swinging the door closed behind her. She stared from Max to the screwdriver in his hand and back again. She didn't have to say another word. After nine years of marriage, he could practically read her mind. *You wouldn't know a Phillips head screwdriver from Phillip's Milk of Magnesia.*

She shook her head, which he interpreted as, *Why am I wasting my life with the likes of you?*

He returned the screwdriver to the drawer and said, "I'll take care of it later. What's up?"

"I know you don't care, but I'm leaving now."

"Leaving?" He couldn't hide the note of exhilaration in his voice. He looked to see if she was carrying a suitcase.

"Don't get your hopes up, Max. It's Wednesday. Remember?"

"Oh, right. Wednesday."

Wanda Sue hit one of the three garage door openers, and walked past him, past his Hummer H2 and climbed into her boxy little Scion. The salesman had told them the official name of the car's finish was Amazon Green, but Max thought a more apt name was Puke Green. Slamming the door closed, she backed out of the garage without another word.

CHAPTER TWO
Wanda Sue and Max

Wanda Sue McClure had grown up on Jacksonville's west side. *The west side is the best side*, she and her girlfriends liked to say. Wanda Sue's brother had been a drummer in a country-rock band for a few years and she watched the band play at neighborhood bars where she was seldom carded since she always looked older than her years. All the boys told her she could easily pass for twenty-one. What they meant, of course, was that Wanda Sue was stacked and delicious looking with her pouty mouth, striking violet eyes and long legs that ended in what she'd been told was "the best looking ass in Duval County." She could walk into any bar and most men found themselves lost in a fog of lust that seemed to trigger instant amnesia. They forgot their inhibitions, and some even forgot they were married.

In her advanced biology class Wanda Sue had learned about pheromones, the chemical scent animals emit resulting in dramatic behavioral changes in other animals. Judging by the swarming males circling her like Jimmy Buffet's sharks schooling around the girl from Cincinnati, she sometimes thought she must possess what she called an IPO pheromone—IPO, standing for *I Put Out*. One whiff and the horny boys had no choice but to erect their fins and hope to take a bite out of Wanda Sue.

But it would be a mistake to judge her solely on her looks. Sure, she hung with the rowdy Westside crowd who thought "Sweet Home Alabama" should be the national anthem. And she'd bestowed her favors on a few of the rock musicians who passed through Jacksonville on their way to Orlando and Miami … though not as many as Max seemed to think.

Wanda Sue kept her intelligence hidden behind a cloak of sex appeal and youthful bravado, but that didn't mean she was some clueless bimbo who'd spend her life behind the counter at the local Wal-Mart. No, she had a plan to live the exciting life of a rock star's wife. Travel. Money. She wanted the complete package—a big house and the reflected fame that came with being married to a rock star.

After high school, Wanda Sue attended the local community college for two years, but the plan was never far from her mind. Each time she went to the Jacksonville Coliseum with her girlfriends she was judging the musicians as potential mates as well as enjoying the music. There were so many possibilities, but it wasn't until she attended one of The Kingslayers' concerts that she zeroed in on Mad Max Gribbins.

The Kingslayers was one of the hottest bands at the time following their Grammy-winning Album of the Year, "Sticks and Stones." Max was the lead guitarist and she liked his dark, mysterious looks, which reminded her of an aging Johnny Depp. On stage he would prance and preen, whipping out guitar chords so fast his fingers were a blur. She also knew Max Gribbins had written many of the band's biggest hits, including their number one smash, *"Never Give Up."*

It took her three-and-a-half years, but Wanda Sue's dream came true. She married a rock star—and how did that turn out, Wanda Sue?

As she drove away from the house, Wanda Sue allowed the old memories to stew in her mind like the first bubbles popping to the surface in a pot of boiling water. A humorless laugh sounding more like a cross between a sneeze and a cough sputtered from her mouth at the thought of how badly she'd misjudged Max Gribbins. He was supposed to be her ticket to perpetual happiness, but it had turned into more of a ticket to perpetual hell.

Not only did he up and quit The Kingslayers two years after they married, but he had apparently pissed away a fortune on God knows what. Oh, she was sure he still had some money stashed away somewhere—which is what kept her hanging around—but Max had to be the cheapest man she'd ever met.

Even though he was still with the band when they built their house in Valencia Park, she had to fight him every step of the way to be sure the house was up to the standards of the lead guitarist of The Kingslayers. She had first lobbied long and hard for them to set up housekeeping in the Los Angeles area, but he fought back just as hard.

"L. A. real estate is ridiculously high," he whined. "California has a state income tax. Do you want to give them half my earnings every year?"

At least that made some sense, but she didn't understand why he worried about taxes when she knew The Kingslayers had been one of the biggest bands on the planet, and Max must have made millions over the years. So they had stayed close to home, building across the river from downtown Jacksonville in the upscale-gated community of Valencia Park.

Living with Max had become one long-running, stress-filled drama after another. When they weren't arguing, he fell into extended silences or complained about the damn Tin Man in his head. Which is why she looked forward to her Wednesday night ritual. Wanda Sue and a few of her old friends would get together at a local bar and talk of old times, ogle the men at the bar, and then go back to their husbands. Or at least that had been her routine until she met Tom Whitlow.

She kicked the little Scion up to fifty and climbed the ramp onto the Buckman Bridge, glad she was going in the opposite direction as most of the afternoon drive motorists returning home after work. The Buckman was notorious for morning and evening gridlock along with frequent fender-benders and an occasional fatality.

She didn't know how much longer she could live with Max. She gazed into the rearview mirror and pushed a lock of her auburn hair off her forehead. At thirty-two, she was still a damn good-looking woman. She needed to start making plans to move on with her life. But first she had to deal with

Max. There was one other thing, and the thought brought a lascivious smile to her lips. There was Tom Whitlow. She hummed a few bars of "Sweet Home Alabama" and merged into the line of traffic.

Max knew Wednesday meant *Girls Night Out* for Wanda Sue and her girlfriends; a trio of former groupies who he felt sure had slept with every rock musician who played the local arena. He'd tapped all four of them, or at least he assumed he did since his memory wasn't what it used to be. He wondered what the girls gossiped about. Did they talk about him? Did they compare one band member to another? And where might he stand in the rankings?

Max loved the life of a rock star, and had done his best to live up to that image during his days with The Kingslayers. Was it his fault girls threw themselves at him and the other band members? It was all part of the life and he wasn't one to turn his back on the rewards that came with having three platinum albums. Of course, it all seemed so surreal to him now, the partying, the groupies, much of it lost in a haze of drugs and booze.

Wanda Sue was different than the other girls. She'd made an impression on him from the very first time he'd seen her in the front row, dancing and shaking her cute little ass at him. Yes, he had to admit she had a great ass along with a fabulous rack, but those eyes are what did him in. They were the most amazing shade of purple he'd ever seen. Shifting subtly in hue depending on the light, from a pale violet to a rich Byzantium, her eyes made it almost impossible to think of anything else whenever she was within ten feet of him.

He liked to think they hit it off right away. The sex was amazing, but that would all change soon after their marriage. Among the litany of horrendous life choices he'd made in his twenty-one years with The Kingslayers—and he wished he could remember all of them for that autobiography he planned to write one day—Wanda Sue was right up there with the worst of them.

Of course, Wanda Sue would tell him he wasn't much of a prize either.

Though Max figured he wasn't any worse than the others of his breed who'd survived the insanity of drugs, sex and rock 'n' roll. Sure, there were multiple drug busts on his record, and so many rounds of rehab they should have named a wing after him. Then there were the paternity suits and his four marriages. He barely remembered his first three wives, but he'd never forget the alimony he still paid and the houses they'd stolen from him.

The Kingslayers had their start in Jacksonville, Florida where most of them played together in high school. Hometown ties were hard to break and the band made a point to play the Jacksonville Coliseum every year, even after they cracked the Billboard Top Ten. Their popularity, like all bands, eventually faded, and the venues and gates grew smaller. Still they enjoyed sellout crowds in Jacksonville, and he could always count on at least one groupie to keep him company after the concerts.

He'd met Wanda Sue when she was nineteen. He was already losing his hearing along with his hair, but Wanda Sue made him feel like they were still on top of the charts, and he was a twenty-five year old stud.

Max had made millions of dollars during the glory days of the band. Most of it went up his nose and who knew where, but after paying for their new house, he'd managed to squirrel away a nice chunk in a retirement portfolio. The investment account was a closely guarded secret. Only he and his financial advisor at Smith Barney knew of the existence of the portfolio with its mutual funds, corporate bonds and annuities. Max had no doubt the only thing keeping Wanda Sue in this loveless marriage was she didn't think Max had any money left to pay alimony. That, and the fact she was content making his life as miserable as possible.

The buzzing in his ears began long before he met Wanda Sue. It started as a high-pitched whining in his left ear, a persistent droning that grew louder after each practice session or concert. Ear protection was unheard of when he first started playing with rock bands as a teenager. The Kingslayers had three guitarists and all of them played with full Marshall stacks cranked up to eleven. Max shunned earplugs until he was in his mid-thirties. By then the damage had been done.

In the beginning the ringing would subside after a few days when he was able to take breaks from playing. But when their first record hit the charts, The Kingslayers were on the road full time and the intermittent whining exploded into a constant clamor. His ears pulsated to an internal beat, whooshing as though his head was filled with water, or in his case, scotch and beer.

Even before they were married, the roaring in his ears had become so distracting it competed with the music he was playing. Waves of high-pitched acoustic cannons caromed inside his head. Unceasing. Intrusive. Max reluctantly accepted the fact he'd lost his ear and his touch. It was time to give up the one thing he ever loved. They'd only been married for two years when he told Wanda Sue he was quitting. She tumbled into a funk so deep and dark Max had to score some anti-depressants to help ease her back to normalcy. He realized that the only reason she'd married him was because he was a member of a popular rock band.

Looking back on it, he couldn't recall if he'd been stoned when she suggested they hitch up. She said she was pregnant and wanted their child to have a regular family. He'd been thinking of leaving the band, and the idea of a little Max to carry on his name, and a young sexpot like Wanda Sue to help ease his retirement made a lot of sense. But so did the time he drank half a bottle of tequila and tried to swim across San Francisco Bay—in February. Fortunately, his mates weren't as stoned and pulled him out.

Max closed his eyes as a current of pain knifed through his head at the thought of his early morning plunge into San Francisco Bay. It brought to mind another more frightening snippet of memory when he'd nearly drowned in the St. Johns River. A kaleidoscope of images tumbled though his head. He was sliding below the surface, inky black water filling his nose and mouth. His arms were slapping the water as he struggled for air and sank lower and lower.

He heard the voice once again and panic seized him as it did each time the repressed memories leaked from whatever recesses of his brain he'd banished them to.

Help me … can't swim … don't leave me here to die

He felt himself sinking deeper into the fetid water. Something gripped his leg, claw-like fingers gouging his skin. He fought to break free, kicking out at the unseen presence, all the while hearing his desperate pleas

… don't leave me here to die

He must have been pleading for his life, but that's where the terrifying recollection always stopped. He knew he nearly drowned in the St. Johns River, but everything else about that night—Why was he in the water? How did he get out?—had been excised from his memory except for ghostly images and fragments of the cries he must have screamed into the night hoping someone would hear his calls for help.

Fortunately, the vision of his near-death experience seldom returned, but it had left him with a lasting souvenir—aquaphobia—a fear of the water. Max had grown up around water, having lived near the beach, but now there was no way he'd ever step a toe into the ocean. Or swim in a pool. He even had trouble sitting in a bathtub.

The Whitlows had a pool in their backyard, and had invited Max and Wanda Sue to share a drink and a swim on numerous occasions. Max usually found an excuse not to go since the sight of that much water usually made him sick to his stomach. Just last week, with April moving rapidly toward May and Northeast Florida enjoying a stretch of unseasonably hot weather, the Whitlows hosted a neighborhood pool party. Despite his reservations, Max agreed to attend after Wanda Sue convinced him he wouldn't be expected to go in the water.

More than twenty people and half-a-dozen kids were there, many whom Max had never met. Keeping his back to the pool, Max tried to ignore the splashing behind him. After a few drinks, he began feeling more comfortable and thought he might survive the ordeal without any real problems.

He looked around to find Wanda Sue and saw her at the shallow end of the pool, a drink in one hand, the other on Tom Whitlow's shoulder. The sun glinted off the blue water forcing Max to squeeze his eyes shut for a moment. He felt a jet of acid attack his stomach lining. When he squinted at the pool again, he saw Whitlow whisper something to Wanda Sue who rewarded him with a smile unlike any Max had seen since he was with The Kingslayers.

Whitlow turned toward him at that very moment, making Max think the man had some kind of radar. He raised a hand to greet Max, his voice rising above the din of the many conversations and noisy children.

"Hey, there, Mad Max. Come on in. You don't have to be afraid, none of us are music critics."

Everyone turned toward Max, laughing and urging him to go into the pool. Max seethed, feeling a wave of heat wash over his face. Wanda Sue must have told him he was afraid of the water. Another reason to hate her, and to add Tom Whitlow to his growing list of people he'd like to see infected with a long, debilitating illness.

It should have been obvious to any idiot that he wasn't there to swim. He was wearing a pair of seventy-five dollar shorts—not a swim suit—an expensive silk sport shirt and French loafers without socks so there would be no doubt swimming was not on his agenda this afternoon.

Max turned away from Whitlow and his wife. He edged a few more feet away from the pool in case Whitlow decided to pull him in. The scent of chlorine tickled his nose. Max's stomach was churning. He was sure his face must have gone gray and they could smell the sweat he felt streaming from his armpits and hear his heart thrumming in his chest.

It took every ounce of strength to control the trembling in his hands, to keep from running away from the indigo water reaching out for him. Max closed his eyes in a futile attempt to keep the chilling images and terrifying voice at bay. But they came back in a flash of repressed memory. The dark waters of the river closing in on him. His cries for help.

… don't leave me here to die

It was too much to take, and he rushed from the Whitlow's backyard toward the safety of his home. As he left, he thought he heard Whitlow and Wanda Sue laughing.

Wanda Sue watched Max scurry away from the party thinking how much he looked like frightened dog, head down, tail tucked between its legs. She was still standing next to Tom Whitlow, who also stared after her husband's retreating body.

"What the hell's wrong with him?" he asked.

She sighed deeply, shaking her head. "There's no telling, but it probably has to do with the pool. I told you he was terrified of water."

"What happened? Did his mother drop him in the tub when she was bathing the widdle baby?" Whitlow snorted and stared into Wanda Sue's hypnotic eyes.

Wanda Sue smiled demurely, cutting her violet eyes across the pool to where Dana Whitlow was surreptitiously surveiling her husband. She was standing with Stan Hampton who was telling her, probably for the twentieth time, about his reign as king of hamburger patties. Everyone was aware of their conversation since Hampton's voice could be heard on the next block.

Hampton lived at the end of the street in one of the biggest McMansions in a neighborhood full of them. Wanda Sue estimated Stan's age to be in the 75 to 80-year range, but despite his advanced age he had many qualities that made him attractive to the right kind of woman. Hampton had retired ten years ago, selling his chain of meat processing plants to Warren Buffett for over a hundred million dollars. She'd Googled him and learned that each of his seven plants processed 500,000 hamburger patties a day along with 200,000 sausage patties. All of them destined for McDonald's restaurants across the country. She thought she could learn to love an older man like Stan Hampton despite his obvious drawbacks, which included a mild case of rosacea that turned his face the color of a ripe tomato, a hearing loss causing him to shout at a decibel level rivaling many of the rock bands she'd followed, and the biggest drawback of all, his twenty-six-year-old trophy wife.

Whitlow followed Wanda Sue's gaze and saw his wife wilting before Stan Hampton's booming voice.

"Better go rescue Dana before Stan deafens the poor girl with his Grade A beef tales." He waded to the pool steps and left Wanda Sue with her thoughts.

She leaned against the side of the pool, welcoming the warm afternoon sun on her face. Tom had upgraded his back yard the previous year with interlocking pavers that set off his Mediterranean style home perfectly. Dotting the perimeter of the pool were plant beds filled with dwarf palms, philodendra, coleus, blooming hibiscus and her favorite, violets,

She closed her eyes and pictured herself on her own tropical island with someone who would love and care for her. As a young girl she had planned her life in exquisite detail, creating a checklist starting with number one—Marry a rich rock musician. She had to admit she had accomplished step one, but since that hadn't worked out so well she needed a new plan. Wanda Sue knew life, like most journeys, was filled with detours and side trips to unexpected places. Her marriage to Max Gribbins was only a bump in the road. A detour.

The next stage of her life would be with a man who could whisk her away to someplace like her fanciful tropical paradise. She thought Stan Hampton could easily fill that role. Hampton didn't fit the image of the handsome stud muffin she'd imagined when she first created her life plan, but Wanda Sue had matured herself and understood there was more to life than good looks and sex appeal. And along with his money, Stan Hampton had another attractive quality: a very short lifespan.

Wanda Sue, you're a terrible person, she told herself, laughing aloud, and then looking around to see if anyone had noticed. She let the image of Stan Hampton and the tropical island drift away replacing it with someone who was more attainable if not as wealthy—Tom Whitlow.

When she first set her sights on Max as the perfect mate, she had yearned—and *yearn* was exactly the word she wrote in her diary. She *yearned* to have Mad Max Gribbins in her arms. She *yearned* to hear him tell her he loved her. She *yearned* to be Mrs. Max Gribbins. She had fallen in lust over Max's dark, brooding good looks and his athleticism in the bedroom. The faint scar on his cheek gave him a dangerous look and she imagined him in a knife fight with a crazy drunk.

Max was also given to long silences, which she believed hid a deep intellect. The yearning ended quickly after she realized Max Gribbins was a self-centered asshole who would never make her happy. And the long silences were not the result of pondering deep philosophical questions with his probing intellect, but the fact he'd destroyed most of his brain cells doing drugs.

So dark and brooding was out. Happy and self-confident in. And tall was an extra benefit she'd learned to appreciate. Tom Whitlow fit all of this and more. He wasn't as rich as Stan Hampton, and honestly, who was, but Tom must be pulling down big bucks from his software business if he could afford to live in Valencia Park.

She let her eyes wander across the pool to where Whitlow and Dana were now talking with another couple, the Abramson's, who lived two houses down and liked to tell anyone who would listen that they'd visited every state in the union and twenty foreign countries. As though an invisible beacon had passed between them, Whitlow turned his head ever so slightly while still nodding at Harv Abramson, who must have been telling them about their latest overseas venture, and caught Wanda Sue's eye. She could see Tom was looking at her and unbidden an image popped into her head so graphic that hot flashes sparked from her breasts, down her stomach and into her groin. If she didn't know better, Wanda Sue was convinced everyone at the pool party was aware of the lurid sexual antics romping through her head at that moment. The picture had been that explicit. That powerful.

Even though she felt herself blushing, Wanda Sue knew her fears were unfounded. The wild sex wasn't happening now—it had happened last Wednesday night.

CHAPTER THREE
Dancing Manatees

The night of the pool party, after he'd run out of Tom Whitlow's backyard like a lost little boy crying for his mother, Max had a nightmare that was just the start of a series of what he came to think of as his own little horror films. In the dream, he had pulled up to the very edge of the river in his Torch Red Chevrolet Corvette convertible, the one that earned Motor Trend's '98 Car of the Year Award. Man, he'd loved that car. It felt like he was riding atop a low-flying hawk each time he wound her up and jetted down the highway. For the life of him, he couldn't remember what happened to it.

Max climbed out of the Corvette, and he must have been fried because everything pulsed and swirled around him in bursts of carnival colors. He heard music, and saw three mariachi musicians standing on a pier overlooking the river serenading the night while a herd of manatees swayed to the music. The manatees were upright, balanced on their paddle-like tails while their flippers slapped together sending gouts of what appeared to be blood into the air where it fell in thousands of red droplets into the river.

The mariachis were dressed in the traditional charro suits, looking like Mexican cowboys with their large sombreros, sparkling waist-length jackets and tight pants. But in Max's dream, they were anything but traditional. They were outlandishly tall and rail thin. Each of the skeletal musicians played a guitar that looked for all the world like the Fender Stratocaster Max played throughout his days with The Kingslayers.

In the dream, the boards of the pier were warped and splintered, but Max walked onto it anyway entranced by the music that had a visual accompaniment of fireworks exploding in the night sky with long tails of red and blue stars. When the musicians saw him they stopped playing and backed away as though Max was infected with some deadly disease.

The middle musician put his hands to his face, his guitar falling first to the floor of the pier, and then sliding magically through the wooden planks into the dark waters of the St. Johns River.

No! No! the musician cried out, and Max saw avocado size tears flowing from his eyes. *You shouldn't be here. Go away*, the musician on the left yelled at him.

Max realized the boards of the pier were cracking even more as he approached the mariachis. Terrified of falling into the river, Max reached out for the handrail only to have it disintegrate in his hands.

Max teetered precariously over the edge of the pier, the inky water below him. Panicked, he stared into the river and saw it change from opaque black into a shade of red matching his Corvette. As he hovered above the water in a strange balancing act that could only happen in dreams, he glimpsed a face bobbing just below the surface of the water. One minute the apparition appeared near the surface, the next it slid away in a tantalizing game of hide and seek.

The face popped up again, this time barely breaking the surface and a spark of recognition touched him, and just as quickly was doused. This went on for what seemed like hours in dreamtime, but was probably only seconds. As the face moved closer, he saw the black hair hanging across one eye. When the specter broke the surface he realized it was a terror-stricken version of his own face. In the dream, Max recoiled in horror as a school of tiny black fish nibbled at the cheeks of the face in the water.

He screamed at the sight even though he knew this was only a dream, and told himself he should wake up. Instead, Max lost his equilibrium and toppled headlong toward the river. But as in many dreams, he was moving in the slowest of motions and the river shifted away from him even as he was falling toward it.

As he hung suspended above the river the mariachi band struck up another tune, but the voice rising from below him drowned it out, echoing familiar words that penetrated his skull louder than any vuvuzelas played by the Tin Man. He recognized the voice as a choked version of his own. It implored him —

Help me ... can't swim ... don't leave me here to die

CHAPTER FOUR
Goodbye Tin Man, Hello Walter Cronkite

Wanda Sue hadn't bothered to close the garage door when she drove off for her Wednesday night outing. Max watched the green Scion turn a corner and disappear. He stood there a moment before walking to the wall switches and hitting the garage door button. It slid smoothly down its track, the chain clicking above him until the door settled against the concrete and silence filled the garage.

Silence! It took Max a few seconds to realize what he was no longer hearing. The ringing in his head had disappeared. The Tin Man was gone.

Max stared dumbly at the garage door motor over his head as though it were a magical talisman that had brought about this miracle. He waited for the ringing to return, unconsciously counting off the noise-free seconds in his head. When he reached 60, he moved into the house, stepping carefully, holding his head as motionless as possible for fear he'd shake something loose, and the familiar racket would reappear.

Inside the house he eased himself into the La-Z-Boy Recliner in the living room. Max closed his eyes, listening to the silence in his head for the first time in twenty years. He'd been living with the Tin Man for so long he didn't know how to react to the peace. To the quiet. His eyelids grew heavy in the silence and he welcomed the sleep that had been evading him for years.

He woke with a start to a darkened house. Still lying on the recliner, Max was confused, not sure where he was. He sat upright remembering the sweet silence. Moving through the kitchen, he saw the illuminated clock on the microwave oven. It was nearly four in the morning. He'd been asleep for almost ten hours. He couldn't remember the last time he slept so long or awakened so refreshed.

Max stumbled into the bedroom. Wanda Sue was curled up on her right side, folded like a contortionist on the edge of the bed as far away from Max's side as she could get without falling off. She hadn't bothered to wake him, and he was thankful for that. Even though he'd slept for ten hours, Max decided it wouldn't hurt to enjoy a few more hours of peaceful sleep. He stripped off his shirt and pants and settled onto the bed. The last thought he had before slipping into another deep sleep was he might check with Cappy to see if he could get his gig back with The Kingslayers.

The smell of coffee woke him. He rolled over and checked the clock radio next to the bed. 9:30. He shook his head in amazement. He'd slept another five hours. But his amazement was tempered with a shocking discovery. The buzzing in his ears was back. He stiffened, clenching his jaw muscles so hard he thought he might crack a molar. He'd hoped he'd somehow been cured, but deep inside knew there was no cure for tinnitus and the blessed silence he'd enjoyed was only an aberration.

Max closed his eyes, acknowledging the bitter truth that he would have to live with the Tin Man's strident blasts for the rest of his life. Even as he accepted the reality of the situation, Max realized something was different about the noise in his head. These weren't the high-intensity whistles and toots the Tin Man had tortured him with for so many years. Instead, he heard a subdued buzzing, more of a murmur than a whine. The humming reminded him of the trimmer his barber used on the back of his neck.

He told himself this was another cruel joke by the neurological gods controlling the electrical impulses flooding his brain. The buzzing in his ears was only a sigh in the wind compared to what he'd lived with for the past two decades, light years from the constant clamor that kept him awake each night. Yet he was afraid to embrace this new condition since he'd only set himself up for a major disappointment when the Tin Man made a return appearance on the big stage in his head.

For the next three days Max monitored the low level sounds, waiting for them to erupt into the familiar unnerving racket. To his wonderment, the Tin Man had seemingly departed, taking his quartet of vuvuzelas with him. Whatever the reason, his tinnitus was noticeably quieter. In fact, the murmurings seemed to be changing with each day that passed. He knew it was crazy, but he thought they were beginning to sound more and more like a whispered monologue. Even though he was unable to make out any words, he was sure the humming had taken on the cadence and pattern of speech.

Was he going insane? The irony of his stage name, *Mad Max*, wasn't lost on him. Maybe the many years of living in a drug-induced cloud had finally caught up with him. He didn't think so, but what else could explain the ghostly whispers he was hearing. He was afraid to share this latest development with Wanda Sue since he knew she'd tell him to check himself into a mental facility. Or, more likely, file a court order to have him committed.

Another more fearful thought struck him: Isn't hearing voices one of the symptoms of a brain tumor?

The whispers continued for two more days, ramping up for a brief moment into a more modulated voice sounding like it was coming through a cheap speaker. Max could only catch a word or two here and there before the voice faded into the background as though the channel frequency had been changed. Words popped in and out of his head, totally out of context, leaving him confused and frustrated. Then they'd melt away. None of it made any sense to him, but the voice became clearer with each broadcast, until he was certain it was a male voice speaking in even, measured tones. Almost like a news announcer.

Max awoke early the next morning, thankful that the voice in his head—he'd named it Walter Cronkite—was silent. Perhaps it was on a commercial break. After a minute of more shadowy, indiscernible murmurs, he felt something pass through his head, almost like a low-voltage shock. Then the ghostly whispers stuttered and he heard a confusing stream of words—"… early …", "… shook …", "… intense …" And as though Walter Cronkite had cleared his throat of an irritating blockage, the voice in his head spun out a complete sentence for the first time.

"A powerful earthquake off the eastern coast of the Philippines knocked out power to several cities and triggered a tsunami alert all along the Pacific Rim."

He sat back in the bed listening to details of the earthquake and the damage it had caused wondering if he had tuned in to the television signals from CNN or Fox News. He'd heard wild stories of people claiming they were picking up radio broadcasts in the fillings of their teeth. He wasn't one of those schizophrenic crazies, but if this continued he'd soon become a basket case.

Max made an appointment to see Dr. Ricchi that very afternoon.

Dr. Anthony Ricchi was an otologist/neurotologist, a specialist in treating ear problems. Max had seen the doctor after his tinnitus was first diagnosed. He was an elderly man with small hands and a pleasant enough face that wore a constant expression of compassion. Behind a pair of wireless glasses, Dr. Ricchi's green eyes seemed to glow with empathy for his patient.

After he told the doctor how the tinnitus had somehow morphed into the nightly news, Dr. Ricchi nodded and gave Max a wry smile.

"I hope your news is better than what we're getting out here in the real world."

"You think this is funny? What if I have a brain tumor? Or maybe I'm going crazy."

Dr. Richhi shook his head, a studious expression replacing the bemused smile of a moment ago.

"I'm sorry. I shouldn't make light of your problem. I don't think it's anything as dire as a brain tumor. But let's make certain." He leaned close and peered into Max's eyes.

"Have you had any seizures, Max?"

"No."

"Any unsteadiness or feeling of falling?"

"Not really."

"How about headaches or double vision?"

"Do hangovers count?" Max said.

Dr. Ricchi laughed and shook his head. "I really don't think you have anything to worry about, but I can certainly schedule you for an MRI if it will make you feel better."

"So, you don't think it's a tumor."

"I really don't. I think what you have is a not so rare condition we call musical ear syndrome."

"Huh?"

"Musical ear syndrome, or MES for short, produces auditory hallucinations. Most often the phenomenon is associated with hearing loss and tinnitus. Your case is a little unusual since MES usually presents as a musical hallucination, but hearing voices is also common among ..." He hesitated and looked rather embarrassed.

"Common among who, doctor?" Max asked.

"Well, it's commonly associated with serious mental illness, schizophrenia. But there are some psychologists who believe that not everyone who hears voices is mentally ill."

"Are you saying I'm going nuts?"

"Not at all, Mr. Gribbins, not at all."

"Couldn't the voices be from a physical problem and not a mental one? Maybe it's a sign of some terrible malignancy growing inside my brain."

Dr. Ricchi's eyes almost twinkled as he patted Max on the shoulder. "I wouldn't worry about that. My diagnosis, considering your history of tinnitus, is that you're suffering from acute MES, which rarely indicates any serious pathology, and it might even go away on its own."

"But you can't be sure, can you?"

"If you want to set your mind at ease about a brain tumor, I can refer you to a neurologist, and provide you with the name of an excellent psychiatrist as well. Otherwise, there's not much I can do for you.

There's something I can do, Max thought, remembering how desperate he was to silence the Tin Man that he was ready to jab a screwdriver in his ear.

"I'd like to tell you we have a miracle cure, Mr. Gribbins, but unfortunately this is one of those cases where modern medicine hasn't been able to offer much in the way of good news. From what you've told me the voice is intermittent, unlike your tinnitus, so at least you don't have to put up with it twenty-four-seven."

"So there's nothing you can do?"

"Some of my colleagues prescribe anti-depressants, but I'm not a big proponent of drugs to treat tinn--"

"It sounds like you're not much of a proponent of anything," Max interjected. "Maybe I should see one of your colleagues who at least are trying to solve the problem."

Dr. Ricchi's expression didn't change. He nodded again, offering the hint of a smile. "I understand your frustrations, Mr. Gribbins, I really do. I've had tinnitus for years. About one in five people develop it. Almost all men will be affected by it as they age, particularly those who have been exposed to loud noises in their youth and followed a rather, uhmm, unorthodox lifestyle."

He paused and allowed himself a slight tilt of the head toward his patient. His green eyes locked on Max's, as though to say, *do you think you might fit this description?*

Max left Dr. Ricchi's office with a prescription for anti-depressants and the names of both the neurologist and the psychiatrist. He didn't know if he'd follow up with either of the specialists or fill the prescription. Driving home he realized that Ricchi was right about the voice being intermittent. He hadn't heard anything from Walter Cronkite since the news about the earthquake this morning, only the undertones of muffled whispers. He figured he could live with that.

He arrived home to find Wanda Sue gone. She was probably playing tennis or shopping with some of her groupie girlfriends. He made himself a roast beef sandwich slathered with mayonnaise and horseradish and topped with a thick slice of red onion. After pouring himself a Guinness Stout, Max took his plate and glass into the den.

He flipped on the TV and switched to CNN to see if there really had been an earthquake in the Philippines. All the news was about the latest budget showdown in Washington. He kept the TV on for twenty minutes while he ate, but there was not a word about the earthquake or the tsunami alert. Finally, Max decided that Walter must be a jazz musician because he was making stuff up as he went.

He clicked off the television and gulped the last of the beer. Before he could pick up his plate and take it to the kitchen, the voice returned. The news report was just as bad as the last one, but this time the disaster had moved to India.

"At least sixty people are dead and scores missing after an overcrowded ferry in eastern India capsized. The accident occurred as the double-decker ferry was approaching shore, Officials fear that as many as one hundred-fifty people were swept downstream or perished in the wreckage."

The newscast went on with more details for another two minutes before it abruptly ended in the middle of a sentence. Max noticed his hands were trembling. He took a deep breath to try to clear the alarming report from his head. It hit too close to home, and he hoped Walter didn't bring him any more disaster stories of people drowning.

"Just my freaking luck," he said to the empty room. "I couldn't get ESPN or MTV. No, I have to tune into TNC, the Tragic News Channel, and put up with the disaster of the day."

He was beginning to think his tinnitus wasn't so bad after all. He put his glass and dish into the sink and grabbed his iPod. Maybe a walk with a little music would make him feel better. At least he wouldn't have to crank up the volume to counteract the Tin Man's cacophony.

It was nearly dark as he walked through the park. The temperature had dropped a few degrees, but he guessed it was still in the mid-70s. With the constant barrage of noise gone, Max could think clearly, and what he was thinking was there had to be a rational explanation for the sudden changes affecting him. He didn't believe in the supernatural. If he couldn't touch, smell, feel or see it with his own eyes, then it didn't exist to Max.

Max was convinced Dr. Ricchi was full of it. These were not simple auditory hallucinations. Where was the music in this *musical ear syndrome?* The voice in his head was rational, organized and completely authentic. It definitely wasn't MES, but he was determined to find out what it was. Isn't that why they invented Google?

He turned toward his house, hoping he wouldn't run into his perky neighbor and his pesky dogs. As soon as that thought entered his mind, Max was struck with an intriguing possibility. Could Whitlow's ham radio hobby with its far-reaching radio waves, somehow percolate these news broadcasts into his brain? He realized this made him sound like a paranoid schizoid, but having been around electronic equipment most of his life he knew they were capable of unusual things.

He hesitated at Whitlow's front door, his finger poised on the doorbell button, unsure of what he would say to his neighbor.

I'm hearing bizarre newscasts in my head, Tom. Have you been tuning in reports of earthquakes and ferry accidents?

How would that make him sound? Like a certifiable lunatic, that's how.

What the hell, he thought and stabbed the button. He waited for thirty seconds, listening for footsteps or any noise from inside Whitlow's house. There was nothing except the yapping of the two dogs. He rang the bell again. When Whitlow didn't answer he knocked on the door. This time, he heard the dogs scratching on the other side and decided Whitlow wasn't home.

Back at his own house Max went straight to his computer and searched for musical ear syndrome. Wikipedia repeated most of what Dr. Ricchi had told him. He read that the composer Robert Schumann was said to have heard entire symphonies in his head. Max believed that. He often heard many of the riffs he'd played during his years with The Kingslayers, but that was different than the news reports he was now hearing.

Max skimmed through different websites, learning more and more about auditory hallucinations. He was amazed to find the phenomenon was far more common than he would have imagined, and that many people considered their voices a positive aspect of their personalities. Still, a majority of medical professionals believed hearing voices was a symptom of some kind of illness or mental heath issue, particularly schizophrenia and manic depression.

Max learned there was even a Hearing Voices Network where people who heard voices got together and discussed their internal commuters. Great, he thought, that's what I need—a Voices Anonymous meeting with my fellow wackos.

Max powered off the computer, more confused than ever. He hadn't read of a case exactly like his, but at least he knew he wasn't alone. He checked the clock and was surprised to see it was nearly 8:00 p.m. His rumbling stomach reminded him he was hungry, and he went to the kitchen to see what surprises awaited him in the freezer. Max sorted through a stack of Wanda Sue's vegetarian meals until he found a "Lumberjack" size roast beef dinner in the freezer and pulled it out along with another bottle of beer from the refrigerator.

Popping the frozen dinner into the microwave, he drank half the bottle of beer waiting for the timer to chime. When the dinner was ready, he placed it on a tray along with a fresh bottle of beer, and moved into the living room. He thought he could learn to live with the voice—just as those other people had done—and found himself anticipating the next broadcast. As he chewed the tough roast beef, the chalky mashed potatoes and the squishy vegetables, he decided his case was definitely unique. Nothing he'd read online resembled the newscasts he'd been hearing. Max decided he should not only embrace the newfound courier in his head, but also document the news reports.

Who knows, I might be able to write a book, maybe sell my story to Hollywood.

After dinner, Max pulled a yellow legal pad from his desk drawer and sat down in his easy chair to await the next report from TNC. He looked at the television set and wondered if he should turn it on and check the news to see if there was any truth to Walter's pronouncements, but decided that would be giving in to his hallucination, and he didn't want to be put in the same category as those nuts who live on industrial strength tranquilizers.

Max had never been one to pay much attention to the news. He didn't read *Time Magazine* or even the newspaper on a regular basis. To this day he didn't watch much television, except for football, MTV and awards show like the Grammys. So he had no idea if there was a ferry accident in India or tsunami in the Pacific.

As he sat in his lounge chair, pad and pen in hand, the ghostly mutterings came alive followed quickly by the same low-level shock he'd felt before the first newscast. Max noted the date and time on his legal pad and waited for Walter's authoritarian voice to report the latest tragedy. He didn't have long to wait.

"Tension in the Middle East ratcheted up another notch today as double suicide bombings shook Tel Aviv."

Max scribbled, Tel Aviv – double suicide bombing.

"Eight people were killed as the attack in a popular downtown café was rapidly followed by another blast in a nearby cinema. Police indicated that at least fifty people were wounded in the attacks."

Max wrote as rapidly as possible as the report continued.

"These attacks followed Monday's bus ambush that killed nine Israeli's near a Jewish settlement on the West Bank. Israel's Defense Minister said the attacks would not go unpunished and promised swift actions against the terrorists."

The report of the Israeli bombings slowly trickled away to mere whispers. Max studied his notes to be sure he'd recorded everything accurately. He was sure he had. And just to confirm the bombings had not taken place, Max clicked on his 73-inch TV and switched to Fox News.

He watched for ten minutes, waiting for a *Breaking News* alert, but there was nothing but more wrangling between the president and Congress. He flipped channels until he found CNN, looking to see if they had any reports of his imaginary news flash. Nothing there either.

Max stared at his notes, wondering if he was documenting his own descent into madness. That would really give Wanda Sue and Whitlow something to laugh about. With that thought, he pictured his ebullient neighbor and Wanda Sue in the pool, her hand on his shoulder, a loving smile on her face he remembered she once shared with him. Maybe they were trying to drive him crazy. Hadn't he seen an old movie with the same premise? Doris Day? Yeah, but he didn't see how they could pull off such a stunt.

With perfect timing, the front door opened and Wanda Sue stumbled in. Literally. Max heard the sound of something hitting the floor—too lightweight to be Wanda Sue—followed by an angry, "Shit!"

He forced himself out of the chair to see what kind of calamity had entered the house along with his wife.

"Are you okay, dear," he said, trying to sound as if he cared.

Wanda Sue leaned against the foyer wall with one shoe in her hand. Two Ann Taylor shopping bags lay on the seagrass rug at her feet.

"That damn rug is dangerous," she said. "I nearly killed myself on it." Her words were a little slurred, and Max realized his wife had combined her two favorite pastimes—shopping and drinking.

"Well, we do have to pick up our little feet when we walk, don't we?" He didn't bother to remind her that she had picked out the rug.

"Screw you," was her rapid and clever comeback.

"I see we've been doing a little shopping. And maybe you stopped off for a little liquid dinner."

She ignored him, scooped up her bags and shuffled into the bedroom.

Max hadn't bothered to tell her that his tinnitus had disappeared only to be replaced by an all news channel reporting a variety of bogus tragedies. He knew it would only give her more ammunition to belittle him. With traces of ghostly whispers skittering through his head, Max decided to call it a day and try to get a good night's sleep.

CHAPTER FIVE
The Mad Max Broadcasting Company

He awoke after 8:00 the next morning and followed the aroma of coffee to the kitchen. He heard the NBC announcer's voice coming from the lanai—as Wanda Sue liked to call the covered porch adjoining the house. He'd spent nearly $25,000 on the outdoor kitchen that was the focal point of the porch. Wanda Sue had insisted on the kitchen when they built the house. She'd also nagged him to build a swimming pool, but Max would sooner have an alligator pit in the bedroom.

His wife sat at the cast aluminum table tucked into one corner of the porch watching the small flat screen TV on a nearby table. The hosts of *The Today Show* bantered about the weather as Wanda Sue forked away at a banana-nut muffin the size of a hubcap.

Max poured himself a cup of coffee and joined his wife on the porch.

"What's got into you?" was Wanda Sue's greeting. "I can't remember the last time you slept in for two days in a row." She broke off another chunk of the muffin and stuffed it in her mouth, signifying she'd had her say on the subject.

Max slurped from his cup before answering. "Just catching up on my sleep deficit. It feels great to get a good night's sleep for a change."

Wanda Sue snorted and went back to watching *The Today Show*, which had switched to a Eurasian-looking woman reading the morning news from the teleprompter. Max decided to move inside and fix himself a decent breakfast for a change. For some reason he craved a ham and cheese omelet with a side of sliced fruit.

He carried his coffee with him, taking three steps toward the French door leading into the house before catching a snippet of a news item from the television. He whirled around to the TV set, spilling a few drops of coffee. Streaming across the screen was a chaotic scene of ambulances and paramedics rushing to help dozens of bloodied victims scattered amongst upturned tables and chairs. In a bold font, a headline across the bottom of the screen read —

Tel Aviv Double Suicide Bombing

In shock, Max listened as the correspondent provided the details.

"… even while medical teams rushed to help the dozens of wounded from the late night café bombing, another suicide bomber brought death and destruction to patrons at a nearby multi-screen theater."

The onscreen video flashed to the front of the movie house where paramedics were assisting a score of bloodied and bandaged people. The correspondent continued, "The bombs were detonated within minutes of one another at approximately ten-thirty p.m. Tel Aviv time, which would be five-thirty this morning eastern time. Authorities indicated that at least eight people were killed and more than fifty wounded."

Max didn't realize his mouth was hanging slightly open and his face had paled by several shades, but he felt his heart pounding as he watched in total disbelief. He'd always assumed that it was only a figure of speech, but he felt the hair on the back of his neck stand out as goose bumps shuttled up his arms.

"What the hell's wrong with you?" his wife asked. "You look like someone stepped on your grave. Do you know someone in Tel Aviv?"

Max ignored her and rushed inside to retrieve the yellow pad. He was sure he'd heard Walter's report of this bombing in the early evening, hours before it was supposed to have taken place. He found the pad in his desk drawer and noted he'd written *Tel Aviv Double Suicide Bombing*, exactly the same as the graphic on the television report. Beneath that was the time—8:42 p.m.

The TV correspondent had said the bombing took place at 10:30 last night, Tel Aviv time, which would have been 5:30 this morning—more than nine hours after the voice in his head relayed the news.

He stared at his notes of the double bombing. It was almost exactly the same as the NBC News report he'd just seen. How was that possible? It wasn't possible, but he was holding the proof in his hands. His head shook involuntarily. No, there had to be a screw-up with the timing. Television news people got things wrong all the time, didn't they? Even though a nine-hour mistake seemed improbable, there couldn't be any other explanation.

Max had lost his appetite. He went into the living room to watch the news, switching from network morning programs to Fox to CNN and back again. Each of them had highlights of the double bombing, and each repeated the same facts as the earlier NBC report, including the time of the bombings. They couldn't all have it wrong, could they?

Totally confused, Max began wondering if he'd imagined the entire thing. Maybe he was totally delusional and he hadn't heard a report about the Tel Aviv bombing at all. But how to explain the notes he'd written last night? The only possible explanation was that he'd written the wrong time. He'd had more than a few beers, and he may have even fallen asleep for a few hours. That had to be it.

He sat back and closed his eyes, suddenly aware his internal murmurings had picked up speed and volume. Walter hadn't made an appearance yet, but he recognized the early warning signs and was sure another of his reports would be along soon. Max hurried to his desk and grabbed a pen. He was prepared to take notes and he wanted to be sure he got it right this time. He wrote down the date and checked both the living room clock and the time flashing on the DVD player beneath the TV. When he felt the buzzing in his head, Walter's cue to start his news broadcast, he wrote 9:17 a.m. and waited for the next tragedy to unfold.

"A member of the Saudi Arabian royal family narrowly escaped assassination today

when a bomb in a parked car exploded as the Saudi Prince's motorcade passed."

Max wrote furiously as the voice continued with more details.

"Prince Mohammed bin Ahmad, a member of the Saudi royal family and recently appointed to the Council of Ministers, was not hurt in the bombing, but three other people were killed. Saudi officials are investigating the assassination attempt, calling it 'an act of terror,' and vowing to find the responsible parties."

The voice drifted away, retreating into the shadowy whispers he'd heard earlier. Max finished writing his notes about the assassination attempt and decided he wanted an omelet after all. If Walter kept to the same schedule, Max wouldn't hear anything more until early evening. He was about to return to the kitchen and start pulling out the ingredients he'd need for his breakfast when the whispers disappeared and his internal newsreader returned. He snatched up the pen and pad again, checked the time and wrote 9:28 a.m.

"The DEA announced this morning it had arrested twenty-five members of a Mexican drug cartel in an early morning raid in a quiet neighborhood in a Tempe, Arizona subdivision. The raid comes at the end of a multi-state and multinational investigation that has been in the works for over six months. DEA Special Agent in Charge Herschel Wilson said his team had seized more than eight tons of marijuana, two hundred pounds of Methamphetamine drugs, nearly three hundred pounds of cocaine and approximately four million dollars in cash."

Max wrote *Mexican Cartel Drug Bust* at the top of the page and noted the amounts of drugs seized along with the 25 cartel members arrested. He made sure to include the DEA agent's name. He waited for more details, but the report fizzled out.

Staring at the notes he'd written, two things struck him immediately. This was the first time the voice in his head had reported two stories in succession, one after the other. And, he realized, unlike all the other reports he'd heard, this wasn't a major tragedy. Maybe Walter had tired of reporting only bad news. He found the prospect of lighter fare encouraging. If this kept up, he'd change the name of his news channel from TNC, the Tragic News Channel, to something more fitting like MMBC, the Mad Max Broadcasting Company.

The next day brought confirmation of both the assassination attempt on the Saudi Prince and the Arizona drug bust. In the meantime, Max's head was streaming with non-stop news reports that kept him scribbling in his yellow pad. The news was a mixture of major events in foreign capitols, and lighter domestic news. In one day he heard about the election of a hard-liner in Israel, a famous Hollywood couple getting divorced and a crane collapse in downtown Cleveland.

He saw verification of each of these the following day. Max was now convinced he was picking up news broadcasts from the future. He didn't understand how or why it was happening to him, but he was sure this was no random auditory hallucination. No matter what Dr. Ricchi might say, he wasn't one of the thousands of walking head cases who heard voices, who joined the Hearing Voices Network or took medication to ease their mental health symptoms. For whatever reason—and he couldn't think of anything that didn't sound like something from *The Twilight Zone*—Max had been given a special gift.

He did more research and learned that people had claimed to divine the future throughout history. Ancient Romans would study the flight of birds to determine if the day was favorable for some action. Others interpreted dreams, while still others read palms or tea leaves or stared into crystal balls. Even Nancy and Ronald Reagan consulted astrologers before making major decisions.

After scrolling through dozens of online pages of nonsensical blathering about divining the future, he found the term clairaudience. He read that clairaudience was a form of clairvoyance, and people with this ability could acquire information by paranormal auditory means. He ignored the explanations about developing this power through Buddhist meditation or causing the *chi* to penetrate the occipital region of the brain as so much new age crap, but at least there were cases of people gaining knowledge through voices only they could hear.

But as much as he searched the web, he couldn't find a single case of anyone hearing news broadcasts from the future. He had never believed in the super-natural, but now Max was beginning to think he was wrong since every single one of the events he'd heard had come true.

Max wasn't one to dwell on the ethics of his new power. What could he do about stopping an earthquake or a suicide bombing halfway across the world? Did he have an obligation to warn people of possible danger? He didn't think so. And who would listen to him, anyway? They'd slap him into a nut house faster than Wanda Sue ran through his savings.

By the end of the week, Max had filled up one entire yellow pad, started on another and was growing tired of the constant stream of news. He never thought he'd miss the Tin Man and his nonstop wailing, but now he was begin-ning to think the tinnitus wasn't as bad as Walter's incessant talking.

His nostalgia for his tinnitus lasted only until he heard the next report.

"In what has been called a giant leap forward in the battle against cancer, Stagenis Pharmaceuticals, the world's largest publically-owned pharmaceutical company, announced successful testing of a new drug extracted from a rare undersea algae. Stagenis CEO Dr. Paul Burton said in a statement that after six years of clinical trials the drug—trade named Cruzinostat—proved to be fifty percent more effective in fighting the most common forms of cancer. The drug is expected to be fast-tracked for approval by the FDA and may go on the market as soon as next year."

Dollar signs began flicking through Max's head as he stared at what he'd just written. Stagenis Pharmaceuticals was real enough. You couldn't watch any news program without seeing a commercial for one of their products, along with the lengthy, unsettling list of possible side effects. He thought the statin medication he'd been taking was a Stagenis product, but they also made a wide range of drugs from insulin medication to Lafidia, their most popular drug which offered men relief for erectile dysfunction for up to 48-hours.

He rushed to his computer and typed in the name of the pharmaceutical company plus the words cancer trials. A listing of the firm's official website popped up along with sub-headings that included *Product Pipeline*. Clicking on the Pipeline link, Max found a chart with nearly fifty compounds undergoing testing. Many were in the registration stage, but others were listed as Phase 1, 2 or 3. Scrolling down near the bottom of the chart Max found Cruzinostat identified as a Phase 3 product.

Max couldn't believe it, but he smiled to himself as he read confirmation of the drug and what Walter's latest report meant. The smile turned into a soft chuckle starting in the back of his throat and spilled over into a laugh he couldn't contain.

"Thank you, Walter Cronkite," he said after he stopped laughing.

He realized this was news he could use. Of course, the medical breakthrough was important for people suffering from cancer, but Max didn't care about the life-saving potential of the drug. All he could think about was how the stock market would react when this news was announced tomorrow. And there was no doubt in his mind it would be a major story on tomorrow morning's newscasts.

He looked at his watch. It was only 2:10 in the afternoon. More than two hours before the market closed. If he was right, and this report followed the same pattern as the other internal broadcasts he'd tracked over the last week, then the big pharmaceutical company would announce its finding in the morning.

Max retreated to his bedroom, found his cell phone and called his broker.

"Russ Collier here," his broker said, sounding a bit distracted.

"Russ, it's Max Gribbins."

"Max, it's been a while. What can I do for you?"

"How much is Stagenis Pharmaceuticals trading for right now?"

"Give me a second," Collier said.

Max heard him punching keys on his computer to pull up the information.

"Here it is. They're at thirty-two dollars and change. You get a hot tip or something?" he said with a laugh. "I have to tell you their financials are pretty strong, but the patent is about to run out on Lifadia and our analysts have them as hold-to-sell. They expect the price to drop to maybe as low as twenty-six or seven."

Thirty-two. Max did some quick calculations. He figured once this news broke the price had to go up by at least four or five points. But what if it turned out to be a bogus report? His palms began to sweat. He had nearly $1,500,000 in his secret portfolio, but he didn't want to fritter any of it away on what amounted to pure speculation.

It's not speculation! Ten stories have come true in the past week, and this one will, too.

He was sure he was right, but the fear of losing any of his secret stash was holding him back.

"Max, are you still there?" Collier's voice cut through his internal debate.

"Yeah, I'm here. I'll tell you what, Russ. Buy five hundred shares of Stagenis for me. Today, before the market closes."

"Max, I've got to tell you I don't think that's a good idea. You've been so conservative with your portfolio, I'd hate to see you—"

Max cut him off. "Don't worry about it, Russ." "You'll get your commission either way, but I have a hunch things will work out okay."

"I sure hope so, Max. I really do."

Sleep eluded Max that night but it wasn't because of any noise or voices in his head. Investing in Stagenis was a big step for him. As Collier had said, he'd always been a very conservative investor. Most of his holdings were in annuities and corporate bonds. He'd stayed away from equities for the same reason he stayed away from roller coasters and swimming pools. He was afraid of anything he couldn't control, and didn't wish to tempt the gods who might be looking to get even with Max Gribbins for whatever sins he'd committed over his life. He knew there were many sins he was aware of, and some he thankfully could no longer remember.

Max finally drifted off to sleep around two in the morning with an image of Walter Cronkite leering at him.

CNBC broke the news in its pre-market *Squawk Box* broadcast at 6:30 a.m. After the anchor read the news of Cruzinostat's successful trials and the pending FDA approval, they cut to a live interview with Stagenis CEO Paul Burton who looked more like a night club owner than the head of a billion dollar pharmaceutical company. His face was fleshy and pale, and he wore heavy black *Buddy Holly* glasses and a thin gray mustache.

"Dr. Burton," the CNBC anchor said, "do you consider this a major breakthrough in the fight against cancer?"

"As you know, Ken," Dr. Burton replied in a surprisingly deep voice, "researchers have been hunting for a magic bullet to combat cancer for a very long time. But it's proven to be elusive primarily because cancer is a complex disease that manifests itself in many ways. Our research spans so many different disciplines, including genetic, diet and environmental factors which impact the mechanisms of carcinogenesis that—"

"Whoa. You'll have to put that into everyday English for me, I'm afraid," the anchor said with a laugh.

"Sorry. Let's just say we haven't had a lot of luck with a global attack on cancer, even though there has been encouraging progress along several different fronts. We believe, however, that our Stagenis researchers have developed the closest thing yet to that magic bullet because it attacks a wide variety of cancers at its source—in the endothelial progenitor cells, which are essential to tumor blood vessel growth."

Burton went on to explain how the new drug battled these cells—he called it an ablation process—and how they hoped to have Cruzinostat on the market within the next two years.

Max felt a rush of anticipation sweep over him as he watched the interview. By God, this was really happening. Like a child lying awake on Christmas Eve, wondering if he'd find a shiny new bike under the tree, Max couldn't wait for the stock market's opening bell.

He'd already seen ample proof his internal news broadcasts were providing genuine glimpses into future events with the Tel Aviv bombings and the attempted assassination of the Saudi prince. But as amazing as those prognostications were … he guessed that was the proper term … *prognostications!* He rolled the word around in his mouth a few times, admiring the way it bounced from his lips to the roof of his mouth to his tongue. He broke it into syllables, saying it aloud, "Prog … nos … ti … ca … tions! Damn, if I'm not a prognosticator."

Back on track, he knew there was a big difference between those other prognostications and what he'd just watched on CNBC. Those events had happened thousands of miles away and hadn't impacted him in the slightest, except to prove he wasn't a certifiable loony cracker. But this new drug had the potential to make him a bundle of money, and that made it deeply personal.

And just as he had hoped, the stock market jumped aboard the Stagenis bandwagon. Over the next three hours he watched the stock price climb from $32.28 to over eighty dollars before settling back to $77.80. Max sat there, the dollars stacking up in his mind. Before the close of the market, he figured he'd cleared $27,500 and kicked himself for not buying more shares.

His cell phone rang and his stockbroker's name popped up on the screen.

"Quite a day, huh, Russ?"

He heard an intake of breath before Russ Collier spoke. "Okay, Max, who's your inside source? There are laws against insider trading, and don't tell me you came up with Stagenis all by yourself." Collier was talking in an urgent tone, but almost in a whisper as though he was afraid someone might be listening to their conversation.

"That's exactly what happened," Max said. *And it was the truth, wasn't it?* "I don't take many pills these days, but I had a cholesterol problem and the doctor prescribed a statin drug."

"Yeah, what—"

"Well, it's manufactured by Stagenis Pharmaceuticals. You might not believe this coming from someone who once swallowed almost any pill or concoction known to man, but now I'm careful about what I put in my mouth. I Googled Stagenis, and—"

"You Googled Stagenis and decided their stock was going to blow through the roof?"

Max ignored the sarcasm and said, "Of course not, but I liked what I saw. The drugs they had in the pipeline looked promising, especially this Crus-i-watcha-ma-call-it. I had a hunch I might be able to make a buck or two and called you. Just dumb luck, Russ. That's all it was."

"Uh huh. Be sure to let me know if you have any more hunches, will you?"

After hanging up Max wondered if old Walter might come bearing any more gifts through the secret voice in his head. He smiled to himself thinking about his investment portfolio growing by another $27,500, and the possibility more might be on its way. The best part of it, he told himself, was that Wanda Sue knew nothing about it, and when they parted ways, which was only a matter of time, he'd have the money all to himself.

CHAPTER SIX
Just A Coincidence?

Max hadn't felt this good in twenty years. His tinnitus was gone, and he was sleeping a solid eight hours a night. As he waited for Walter's next broadcast, Max pulled his old ax out of the closet, plugged in the amp and began strumming. His fingers felt tight and cramped as though they belonged to a much older man, but as he went through the string progressions practicing some of his old techniques—pull-offs, vibrato and hammer-offs—it all came back to him. He threw in a few power chords before slipping into the first break from Eric Clapton's solo on "Crossroads," kicking it up a notch and feeling the old power surge into his hands and arms.

He glanced up and saw Wanda Sue standing in the doorway, one hand tapping the doorframe, her head bobbing to the Clapton classic. He smiled at her and kept playing.

An hour later Max and Wanda Sue were sitting on the porch eating lunch. Another first, Max thought. Although they lived in the same house, they'd fallen into different patterns of their day-to-day lives. It had been some time since they actually sat down together for a full meal.

"Damn, Max, I hate to say this but you sounded good. Almost like old times."

Max didn't have any trouble believing Wanda Sue hated to compliment him, but then he hadn't given her much to compliment him about. "It did sound good, didn't it? Felt good, too,"

"Do you think you might …" Her voice trailed off.

"Might what? Join another band? Get my old gig back?" He snorted at her unspoken suggestion. Although Max liked to think he still had the chops to front another band, he knew his time had passed.

"Those days are long gone. Neither of us are kids anymore, and I'm not sure I'd want to return to the old life again, anyway."

"Stupid idea, huh?" Wanda Sue said. "Must have lost my mind there for a minute thinking you could do anything but sit around the house all day and feel sorry for yourself."

She picked up her plate and glass and walked inside the house without another word.

Nearly twenty-four hours had passed since the news about the Stagenis cancer drug, and Max was beginning to worry. For the past two weeks he'd been receiving three or four news reports a day. Now his head was clear of the ghostly whispers, leaving only obsessive thoughts roiling through his brain.

Could he have heard the last report of things yet to come? The thought of a life without Walter's comforting voice left him feeling somehow empty, as though someone he cared deeply about had died unexpectedly.

He went to bed that night without hearing a single report. Not a murmur or a whisper. Somehow he was able to sleep, but the dream returned to him and he was back on the pier with the three gaunt mariachis. As he approached them, he noticed for the first time their skin was swollen and wrinkled, and a fine white froth bubbled from their lips.

Stay away … one of the musicians screamed at him. Max backed toward the railing, as he had in the other dreams. And once again the railing dissolved. He tumbled forward, his arms windmilling. This time the thing in the water reached out for him. He saw its fingernails were painted black and as he hung suspended above the water the fingers grew longer and fatter, slithering toward him like a swarm of eels.

He knew he was dreaming yet he couldn't help screaming as the freakish fingers inched closer and closer. His terror-filled wails echoed across the river while the mariachi band struck up a Latin version of Ozzy Osbourne's "Let Me Hear You Scream."

The fearful voice returned, insinuating its way into his head, caroming like a pinball bouncing from post to post and firing off neurons in his brain. By now he knew each word by heart. The same words. The same phrase every time.

Help me … can't swim … don't leave me here to die

In the dream Max was no longer suspended above the water but falling toward it in the same slow motion movement that occupies so many dreams … and below the water the open eyes of his dead face stared at him vacantly. It struck him then that the eyes were blue. Max knew his eyes were brown. And as the water rippled over the face, the black hair turned into long blonde tresses. His sharp, masculine features softened and it became the face of a young girl. A young girl with horrific eel-like fingers reaching out to Max's falling body. It seemed to him each fingertip was like the head of an eel with probing black eyes and a mouth filled with tiny pointed teeth.

The closer the fingers came, the louder he screamed until he felt their cold wet tips brushing over his arm. The girl's face loomed larger and larger, and he saw her nose had been broken. It was twisted to one side and dried blood caked along the bridge of the nose.

Max awoke covered with sweat, not river water. He guessed he hadn't actually screamed aloud since Wanda Sue was still snoring on the other side of the king-size bed. The dream was a manifestation of the fearful images he'd had since he nearly drowned in the St. Johns River, an event that must have shaken him so badly he'd repressed much of it from his memory. Every recurrence of the dream left him shaken, but he didn't know what to make of the latest variation where his face had transformed itself into that of a young girl.

He stumbled out of bed, shambling to the adjoining bathroom. It was only 6:00 a.m. but he knew returning to sleep was out of the question. Even if he was able to fall asleep, he wasn't about to chance slipping into the nightmare world again. A world where manatees danced on their tails and dead girls reached out to him. No, he'd take his chances on this side of consciousness and wait for his favorite announcer to deliver tomorrow's news.

Max drank two cups of coffee while watching CNBC. Stagenis' incredible jump in value was still headline news. The big Pharm's stock price had more than doubled in one day's trading. One analyst believed it would continue to climb, while another cautioned there might be a market correction in the coming days. Max made a mental note to call Russ with a stop-loss order in case the second analyst was right. He seldom ventured into the stock market because of its volatility. It seemed to him the market was a fickle and unpredictable creature, rising or falling at the mere hint of good or bad news. All that had changed now because of Walter's reports, but he still wouldn't take a chance on losing any of his lucky windfall.

Before he called his broker, Max heard the familiar static tickling his ears followed by the low murmurings that signaled the start of another of Uncle Walter's big announcements.

Max hustled back into the house, moving swiftly to his office chair where he kept the legal pad with his notes. Somewhere in the distance, a lawnmower was buzzing through a neighbor's yard. He heard the tinkle of dishes in the kitchen as Wanda Sue prepared her breakfast. He gripped the pen tightly, prepared to record tomorrow's breaking news, especially if it helped him make more money.

His head hummed for a moment, and then the familiar spoke.

"In a shocking development, Stagenis Pharmaceuticals CEO, Dr. Paul Burton, was rushed to a St. Louis hospital this morning after he collapsed at a staff meeting. Just yesterday, Dr. Burton announced a major breakthrough in the fight against cancer with the successful trials of its newest wonder drug, Cruzinostat."

There was a pause in the transmission, and Max held his breath waiting to hear the rest of the story.

"We've just learned that Dr. Burton has died from a brain aneurism. Stagenis Board Chairman H. J. Lawson has released the following statement:

We are deeply saddened to announce that Paul Burton passed away this morning. Paul's brilliance, passion and boundless energy guided Stagenis over the past fifteen years, helping to improve the health of people all over the world. Paul's dream of making diseases like cancer a thing of the past is becoming reality thanks to his good work. It's a fitting tribute that he was able to announce the latest and most effective weapon yet in the battle against this deadly disease. Our hearts go out to Elaine and his family, and to everyone who was touched by this extraordinary man.'

Max stared dumbly at the blank page. He hadn't written a word as he listened unbelieving to the report of Burton's death. He dropped the pen and watched it bounce once and roll off the desk onto the floor. He didn't know the Stagenis CEO, had never heard of him before yesterday, yet somehow he felt a kinship he couldn't explain.

He sat unmoving for a few minutes contemplating the frailty of life before he had another, more urgent thought. How would this affect Stagenis' stock? Christ, why hadn't he put in the stop-loss order before this? And then he remembered he was the only person in the world who knew Paul Burton was living on borrowed time and would be dead tomorrow.

Max grabbed his phone, called Russ Collier's office and put in the stop-loss order.

Four hours later the whispers returned, and Max waited for the next announcement from his secret voice. Burton's death was still on his mind and he hoped he hadn't switched channels back to TNC—the Tragic News Channel. He listened carefully, as the announcer began his report.

"U. S. Federal Reserve Chairman Jonathon Montgomery appeared before a Congressional Commerce Committee in Washington today warning of the possibility of another deep recession. He cited the fact that both the Greek and Italian economy appear to be on the verge of collapse and European Union leaders are unable to come to an agreement on how to fix the problem. Montgomery said it might take months to stabilize European markets.

An immediate surge in the price of gold followed his remarks as investors look to shelter their holdings and speculators drive the price of gold even higher. The price of gold set a one-day record, rising an unprecedented $125 an ounce to $2,123.

Oakmont Mining Corporation, owner of the country's largest producing gold mines, has ramped up production in all of its open-pit mines and the five underground ones near Elko, Nevada. A spokesman for Oakmont said they were adding additional shifts of workers to meet the demand."

The voice retreated until Max heard only unintelligible whispers and soon that was gone. He examined his notes, underlining the phrase ... *rising an unprecedented $125 an ounce.* He'd never had the nerve to invest in commodities or metals like gold and silver, thinking them too risky, but the odds had definitely changed in his favor. He put down his pen and picked up the phone.

Collier thought he was crazy when Max told him he wanted to buy gold.

With a sigh—and Max could picture the stockbroker shaking his head—Collier said, "What do you have in mind, Max? You don't want the actual bullion, do you?"

Max couldn't imagine having to worry about storing a bar of gold. "What are my options, Russ? What would you suggest?"

"Some people like to own physical bullion. You can buy a one-kilo bar, which is about 32 ounces, or smaller size bars. There are also a few mutual funds and ETFs that specialize in gold and silver, but I'd suggest going with gold stocks."

Collier paused, and Max thought he heard him hitting the keys of his computer.

"Some of the mining companies look very attractive now, but I have to tell you, Max, the demand for gold has been falling and most people are selling instead of buying."

"What about Oakmont?" Max said.

"You've done your homework, I see. Oakmont's one of the biggest producers of gold in this country, but their stock is down about twenty-percent over the past year. You can pick them up for $30.12 a share."

Max did a quick calculation on his pad, dividing the $27,500 he'd made from the Stagenis stock by $30. "Oakmont sounds good to me, Russ. How about buying me nine hundred shares today?" He put special emphasis on the last word.

"Nine hundred shares? Are you sure you want to risk that?"

"Yes, I'm sure," Max replied.

"I have to ask you, Max, is this another one of your hunches? You've always been a very conservative investor as long as we've worked together. It's my job to advise you, and I think you're stepping out on a limb with this purchase."

"Hey, I appreciate the warning, I really do, but I've done some research on it and feel gold is about to turn around. Go ahead and place the order and we'll see what happens in the next day or so. If the stock price happens to go up I'll want to place another stop-loss order to protect myself."

Collier agreed and said he'd email him with details of the buy. Before he hung up, the stockbroker said, "Wasn't that the craziest thing about the Stagenis CEO dying like that? You buy the stock one day, and the next day he's dead. Lucky you put that stop-loss order in when you did."

"Crazy for sure. Goes to show you never know when your time is up."

As Walter had predicted, Montgomery's dire warning was met by a rapid fall in the stock market and an immediate jump in the price of gold. By the end of the day, Oakmont's stock had risen to $61.44 and Max had made a sweet profit of over $28,000. Elated, he spent the rest of the day playing his guitar and grinning like an idiot.

When Wanda Sue commented on his happy disposition, he told her it must be the music because he'd never felt better and everything was looking good now, even her.

She peered at him for a minute as though trying to figure out if he was using again, shook her head and left the room.

Over the next three days Max's personal news channel filled his head with what he considered mundane and inconsequential reports. There was a gas leak in Duluth that demolished an apartment building, the closing of a major bookstore chain, a wildfire in California and a Miami city official indicted for bribery. But he didn't see how to make money from any of it and his interest began to wane. Wednesday morning's broadcast grabbed his attention once again.

"A small earthquake in northern Nevada triggered an underground rock fall at a gold mine near the remote town of Elko, between Reno and Salt Lake City. Officials of the Oakmont Mining Corporation, owners of the Sierra Madre Mine, released a statement indicating the earthquake caused a significant cave-in and at least thirty-six miners are trapped at the 2,500-foot level. A company spokesman reports they've been unable to communicate with any of the trapped miners, but rescue operations have begun."

Max felt sick to his stomach. His heart was racing as he pictured tons of rock falling onto the miners. Could it be his old friend Walter Cronkite was just messing with his head? First he bought the Stagenis stock, pocketed an easy $27,500 and what happens? The CEO of the company keels over with a brain aneurism. Then this gold mine tragedy.

Max believed coincidences happened, but this was too uncanny. He began pacing around his office trying to make sense of it. It had to be a coincidence. Had to be. The double tragedy nagged at him until he decided there was nothing he could do about any of it. The events had occurred hundreds of miles from his home in Valencia Park. Paul Burton had died in St. Louis, and the mine collapse was in Nevada.

Hey, I'm not the Grim Reaper. I don't control when people die.

That made a lot of sense to Max. Satisfied, he went to the kitchen to wash the dryness out of his throat with a beer.

April had slipped away and most of the first week of May went by without any real news. Max had nearly tuned out of what he considered the same useless crap that caused him to stop watching the evening news years before. That Friday proved to be different, as Walter brought him an item from the sports world.

"In what has been called one of the greatest upsets in Kentucky Derby history, Whiskey Sour, entering the race at eighty-eight to one, emerged from nowhere to pull ahead of the favorite, Strike A Pose, to win the 139th Run for the Roses. Jockey Pedro Alamedas rode

the gelding from far back to score a dramatic half-length victory over Strike A Pose, who entered the race at even odds.

Whiskey Sour's trainer, Bill Schumacher, was seen with tears in his eyes after the race as he embraced first the winning horse and then the jockey. Schumacher said it had always been his dream to win a Kentucky Derby since he began working with horses nearly forty years ago."

As the news announcer continued with more details of the race, Max turned his attention to his calculator. At 88 to 1, he would make $88 for every dollar he bet. His head spun with the thought of a huge payday for very little investment. This would make the profits from his two stock purchases seem like chump change. A $1,000 bet would net him over $88,000 dollars.

He immediately saw the possibilities for an even bigger jackpot. Why not bet $10,000 or even $50,000. His head swam picturing a stack of dollar bills totaling $4,400,000. But just as quickly he realized how such a bet would look on an 88 to 1 horse. It would surely raise the curiosity of Derby security officials. And he didn't want to explain to anyone about the voice in his head. Not that they'd believe him, but that was just as bad since they might accuse him of participating in a conspiracy and invalidate his bet.

In the end he decided betting $2,500 would probably raise fewer questions, and he'd be more than happy with the $220,000 payday. The only problem was he had no idea how to place a bet on the race. He didn't know any bookies, but figured horse race betting must be legal since South Florida's Gulfstream Park was one of the best-known tracks in the country. A search of the Internet told him he could bet on any horse race and do it at his local dog track.

That afternoon he withdrew $2,500 from his market fund and drove to a nearby dog track. Standing in a long line at the Pari-Mutuel window, Max fidgeted and pulled at the neck of his polo shirt, which seemed to have shrunk several sizes in the past few minutes. He kept one hand in his pants pocket clinging to the wad of cash.

They'll know something is wrong if I bet all this money on an 88 to 1 horse.

What if he calls security?

Max's head was reeling and he was ready to bolt from the line when the cashier yelled, "Next."

The man behind the window barely glanced at him when he placed the bet on Whiskey Sour to win, and passed him the $2,500. Max forced a laugh and asked Dan, identified by the nametag on his shirt, "If lightning strikes and this old nag actually wins, do I show up here with a wheelbarrow or will you mail me a check?"

Dan cast a bored look at him as he handed him his ticket. "We pay a maximum of $5,000 in cash and you'll get a check for the rest. After Uncle Sam gets his cut, of course."

He looked past Max and said, "Next."

After Whiskey Sour won the Kentucky Derby, Max waited impatiently for the other shoe to drop. Hadn't recent history shown him his good luck meant bad luck for someone else? Apparently a karmic price tag was attached to each dollar he collected. Even though he told himself he wasn't to blame for the deaths of Burton and the miners, deep inside Max felt he must be somehow tied to the awful things that happened to these people.

As he listened to Walter's daily newscasts, he expected to hear of another tragedy tied to the Derby race. But there was no news on Sunday, Monday, Tuesday or most of Wednesday, and Max let himself believe the jinx had been snapped. Wednesday evening's report was like a slap in the face, snapping Max back to grim reality.

"Five days ago Kentucky Derby winner Whiskey Sour was riding high. Back home at his Ocala, Florida farm, his handlers were preparing him for the next stage of the Triple Crown with his first timed workout since Saturday's big race. As he approached the turn, according to witnesses, Whiskey Sour broke a leg and had to be euthanized. Today, both the surprising gelding that came out of nowhere to beat an odds-on favorite is dead along with his trainer, Bill Schumacher.

In what is being called a bizarre and horrifying series of events, Schumacher rushed to his horse's side after the accident and apparently suffered a massive heart attack. Authorities are investigating rumors that the horse had been receiving intravenous injections of potent drugs for pain and a possible joint disorder."

Max Gribbins could only shake his head at the news. He could no longer call them tragic coincidences. He didn't understand why it was happening, but was convinced there must be a cause and effect between his profiteering and the unintended consequences. The first two incidents were far away from him and though he felt sorry for the victims, Max was happy to accept his end of the consequences.

This tragedy with the Derby winner and his trainer had moved a little too close to home for his comfort, however. Ocala was about two-and-a-half hours from Valencia Park. Maybe it was time to sit on his winnings and let Russ Collier multiply them through the magic of compound interest.

CHAPTER SEVEN
Going Postal

Wanda Sue inhaled deeply, enjoying the rich scent from the jasmine shrubs in Tom's yard. A lurid thought of what the two of them had done last Wednesday night flickered across her mind and brought a smile to her face. One day soon, she hoped, she'd be rid of Max and Tom will have done the same with Dana. Then they wouldn't have to sneak around like lovesick teenagers anymore.

She pulled a handful of envelopes and circulars from the mailbox in the front of their home, sorting through the usual assortment of bills and junk mail. She almost flipped past a large white envelope from Morgan Stanley Smith Barney addressed to Max. About the only mail she remembered Max receiving from financial management firms were solicitations to attend investment and retirement seminars. Something about the envelope told her this wasn't a solicitation. There were no slick marketing slogans across the front … *Jump Start Your Retirement! … Dinner's On Us When You Sign Up For Our Seminar!*

No, this looked like an official correspondence similar to the royalty statements Max received. It was just a plain white envelope with the Smith Barney logo at the top left corner and Max's name and address behind the little window. It could be nothing, but it had some heft to it so she knew there were at least four or five pages inside. And the clincher was the string of three letters and six numbers next to his name.

She tore the envelope open with her finger and pulled out six pages filled with columns of numbers. Wanda Sue may not have been familiar with financial statements quite like this one, but she immediately recognized the quarterly statement for what it was. But what caused her eyes to widen was the line on page one that read *Total Value of Your Portfolio: $1,487,669.93.*

"You son-of-a-bitch," she said aloud.

All this time Max had been telling her he'd pissed away most of his money during his time with The Kingslayers. And she'd been stupid enough to believe him considering his lifestyle and three divorces. Sure, he still had enough to buy the house, with money in reserve to pay their bills. Then there were the royalty checks from record sales so she knew they weren't suffering, but he'd hidden over a million dollars from her and she didn't like it. Not one bit.

A sly smile slid across Wanda Sue's face. Won't Max be surprised when my attorney springs this on him? He'll be singing an entirely different song when he finds out he's going to lose everything in the divorce.

Wanda Sue had been talking with one of the best divorce attorney's in Northeast Florida, but she hadn't wanted to pull the trigger until Tom divorced his wife. He'd been making vague promises for months, but so far nothing had happened except their weekly shack-ups.

The question now was what to do with her newfound knowledge. Should she confront Max with it or put the statement away and use it as additional ammunition during the divorce proceedings? She glanced over at Tom's house wondering what his advice would be. Dana Whitlow was out of town, as always, but Wanda Sue wouldn't take a chance that Max might see her going into their neighbor's house. Instead she walked in the other direction, pulled her cell phone from her pocket, found Tom's number and tapped the Call button as she walked.

"Hey, babe," Whitlow said almost immediately. "Did you want to come over for a quickie?"

"That's tempting, Tom, but I have something to tell you, and I want your opinion on what I should do about it."

She looked at the open statement in her other hand. There were multiple columns listing all the investment products in her husband's portfolio along with pie charts graphing the account allocations.

"That sound's serious. What's up?"

Wanda Sue told him about finding the Smith Barney statement; the fact Max had been hiding an investment portfolio from her. "An investment portfolio of a million-and-a-half dollars."

Tom blew a low whistle into the phone. "That son-of-a-bitch isn't as dumb as he looks."

"That's not saying much, but what do you think I should do? I could save this until our lawyers sit down together and spring it on him then. I'd love to watch all the color drain out of his smug face when he realizes he's going to lose a big portion of his hidden treasure."

Again, the line was quiet and Wanda Sue waited for a response. "Well? What do you think," she finally said, the impatience reflected in her voice.

"I'll tell you what I'd do in your place. I'd be so pissed off at his duplicity, at the fact he had so little respect for his own wife that he'd keep her in the dark like a mushroom, that I'd march right in there and slap him in the face with that statement."

"You think that's a good idea?"

"Hell, yes. Let him know he can't get away with that kind of crap. That you're on to him and when the time comes you're going to walk away with everything, and all he'll have left is his stupid guitars."

"No he won't. I think I'll take those, as well."

"That's the spirit. He obviously holds you in contempt if he does this sort of thing. He doesn't value you. Doesn't love you. And certainly isn't planning to share anything with you."

Wanda Sue felt the anger growing inside her like a bubbling cauldron of steam sizzling in her belly and spreading through her chest.

"Wanda Sue," Tom said, "you have to show him he can't get away with this kind of shit anymore. Where are you now?"

"I'm walking north. Maybe two blocks from the house."

"Turn around. Go back home and tell him what you think of him."

And Wanda Sue did.

As soon as Wanda Sue stormed through the front door, Max sensed trouble. She was waving a fistful of papers at him and cursing him with words he'd never heard her use before. She stopped inches from where he was sitting in the den watching television. He immediately jumped to his feet for a better defensive position.

"You conniving sonuvabitch," she shouted.

"What are you talk—?"

She didn't let him complete the sentence, but slapped him across the side of the head with the papers.

"This is what I'm talking about. This!" And she swatted him again.

Max grabbed her wrist to keep her from inflicting any more damage. "Settle down, Wanda Sue. What the hell's gotten into you?"

She took a deep breath and he saw she was trying to regain control. When she seemed to relax, he released her wrist. "Now tell me what's going on."

She answered him with another whack to the head, this time with her entire hand, not just the papers.

Max stepped back and put up his hands to ward off any more blows. She kept coming.

"All this time we've been married you've been the cheapest bastard, always whining about how we have to keep our expenses low, how we can't buy this, we can't buy that because you'd lost most of your money." She paused and gasped down another deep breath, her chest heaving with anger.

Max had a bad feeling where this was going, but kept to his story. "I know you thought you'd married this rich rock star, but as I told you a hundred times—maybe a thousand times—I went through almost all of my concert and record earnings. We had to be a little frugal if we—"

"What a load of crap. I always suspected you were lying through your teeth, but now I have the proof."

She waggled the sheaf of papers in his face. This time Max caught a glimpse of the Smith Barney logo and the words, Quarterly Statement.

"I can … I can explain …" he stuttered.

Wanda Sue stood with her legs apart, fists on hips, looking like sparks might fly from her violet eyes and smoke pour from her ears.

"Go ahead and explain why you hid an account of a million-and-a-half dollars from me. You might as well rehearse your answer now, Max, because you'll be telling it to my lawyer and the judge after I file my divorce papers."

"Now, hold on Wanda Sue. Don't do anything hasty. That account is our nest egg. It's going to get us through our golden years of marriage. I … I was going to surprise you with it on our … tenth anniversary." *Can she be stupid enough to buy this pile of horseshit?*

"That is the biggest pile of horseshit I've ever heard," she said, as if reading his mind. "You'd better come up with a better story than that by the time the lawyers start dividing the assets because I don't intend to leave you with anything except some of your old guitar strings."

"But Wanda Sue," Max said, attempting to keep the anger from his voice, "we can work through this without any lawyers. Just give me a chance to show how much I love you."

He was worried his nose might have grown a few inches with that last lie, but Wanda Sue had already whirled away from him and stalked off toward the bedroom. The door slamming was her final statement on the subject.

His heart was beating so rapidly, Max thought he was having a heart attack. He dropped into his chair and put his head down, fearing he might faint. He'd been divorced three times already, and while none of them had been especially pleasant, he had the feeling this one would set the bar for wretched divorces so high they'd write books about it.

When his heart rate returned to near normal, Max found his cell phone and stepped out to the porch and called his broker.

"Russ Collier. How can I help you?"

"It's too damn late to help me, Russ. You've screwed up my life for good."

"Max, is that you? What's the problem, my friend? Did you run out of hunches?"

Russ gave a little laugh but Max wasn't smiling. "I'll tell you the problem. You sent the quarterly statement to my house. To my house, for Christ's sake!" His voice cracked as he screamed out the last sentence.

"Whoa, settle down, Max. You're a bit overwrought."

Max drew a huge gulp of air and held it for twenty seconds before releasing it slowly through his mouth. When he felt he could continue, he said, "How many times did I tell you that I didn't want anything sent to the house. That this was a personal account and all correspondence was to go only to my post office box or electronically to my computer? You remember that, don't you?"

"Sure, Max. And that's exactly what we've done. There must be some mist—"

He stopped abruptly, and Max thought the line had gone dead.

"Russ?"

"Yeah. Give me a minute. I'll be right back."

This time the line did go dead except for a string orchestra playing the old Neil Sedaka hit, "Breakin Up Is Hard To Do." That's just perfect, Max thought. He waited for two minutes trying to ignore the cloying music.

"Are you still there, Max?"

"I'm here. What's going on?"

"I owe you a big apology, pal. Rachel, my longtime assistant moved to Virginia with her new husband last week and I have a new assistant. I'm afraid she sent the statement to your house by mistake." He paused, cleared his throat, and said, "It was an honest mistake, Max. She wasn't aware of your special circumstances. Is there anything I can do to make up for it?"

"Do you want to pay for my divorce?"

CHAPTER EIGHT
Walter to the Rescue

Max spent the rest of the day alternately trying to communicate with Wanda Sue through the closed bedroom door and wondering what the hell he was going to do. He couldn't afford another divorce, especially now that his wife had learned about his secret investment portfolio. Everything had been going so well over the past few weeks. Not between Wanda Sue and him, of course, but with the money he'd made from the voice in his head. Particularly that last one on the Kentucky Derby winner.

If he couldn't work it out with his wife, at least he still had the voice and maybe it would make him more money. But there was no guarantee Walter would stay with him. His tinnitus had disappeared, and so could these weird newscasts. Or they might change to a music station playing old Mitch Miller hits with the way his luck was going.

He drank his dinner that night and stumbled into one of the guest bedrooms around 10:30 since Wanda Sue was still barricaded in their bedroom. He spent a fitful night, tossing one way and then the other. When he did manage to sleep his old nightmare returned complete with the cadaverous mariachi and dancing manatees.

He'd awakened at 5:15 and lay there for the next hour, no closer to an answer than when he went to bed. He went to the bathroom, washed his face and hands and decided to make breakfast.

Preparing a pot of coffee, he optimistically placed two cups on the table, and began pulling out the ingredients for blueberry pancakes, one of Wanda Sue's favorite breakfast meals. When the coffee finished brewing he poured two cups, taking one to the bedroom. He tapped on the door.

"Honey, here's your coffee. I'm making blueberry pancakes. They'll be ready in no time."

He listened for a reply and thought he heard some movement behind the door.

"I've got your coffee right here if you want it."

He smiled as he heard the lock click and the door open. But the smile faded as Wanda Sue's arm reached through the partially open door, snagged the coffee cup from him before shutting the door again.

Huh. I wonder if that means she doesn't want any pancakes.

Max decided he wanted pancakes and cooked up two stacks, leaving one on the stove while devouring the other. He couldn't remember being so hungry in the morning. Maybe that was a good sign. Or maybe it was his body's way of storing up food while he could still afford to buy it.

Max opened the French doors to the porch hoping a change of scenery would miraculously spark some brilliant solution to his problem. He had no way of knowing that he'd hear a solution within minutes.

When the familiar whispers began flitting through his head, Max awaited the imminent arrival of another news broadcast. He hurried to his office, prepared to welcome the gravely voice of his newsreader. Max wondered if this report might presage another stock tip or a winning sporting event that would add more dollars to his portfolio. Then he remembered it was no longer *his* portfolio since Wanda Sue would surely walk away with at least half of it, but that didn't mean he couldn't profit from any new prognostications.

Seconds later he heard Uncle Walter's voice.

"Florida Highway Patrol and county deputies are investigating an accident on the Buckman Bridge this morning that apparently claimed the life of a woman who plunged over the railing into the St. Johns River. According to witnesses on the scene, a Ford Expedition swerved to avoid a stalled vehicle and collided with a green Scion. The Expedition sent the

smaller vehicle hurtling across two lanes of traffic, where, in the words of one witness, 'it took a nose dive over the guard rail and into the water.'

The accident happened at approximately 8:30 this morning, tying up traffic for hours as workers cleared the wreckage and attempted to pull the car from the river. Divers from the Sheriff's Department have recovered the woman's body and she has been identified as thirty-two year-old Wanda Sue Gribbins.

More details to follow."

"Oh, shit." The words spilled from a mouth that had suddenly gone dry. Max felt like his heart was about to leap from his chest. He couldn't believe what he'd just heard. Wanda Sue was going to die tomorrow morning. That damn bridge had been the death of more than one person, but Wanda Sue? Wild and worrisome thoughts were coiling through his mind like a nest of snakes knotted around one another, hissing and biting.

He ran a hand through his thinning hair and felt the tremor in his fingers. *I guess this is what they call a quandary.* Sure, Wanda Sue had made his life miserable and she was about to take him to the cleaners, but he couldn't let her drive across that bridge without warning her.

Could he?

Hey, Max, my boy, get a grip. A few minutes ago you were crying in your coffee, searching for a miracle solution. Well, don't tell me prayers aren't answered.

But this is so damn cold, he argued with his darker side. She is my wife and I owe it to her to … He stopped his internal debate, realizing he didn't owe Wanda Sue anything. She was the one who owed him. He had taken in this … this groupie … no better than a trailer trash slut. She enjoyed the prestige of being married to me Mad Max, a fucking rock star. And what do I get in return? Nothing but grief, and a threat to steal me blind. Leave me alone and broke.

Max decided to let nature take its course. After all, the voice in his head was an aberration. He didn't believe in predestination, and no one really knows what the future holds. The day and time of our passing was in the hands of fate or ill fortune, or whatever god you believed in. It certainly wasn't his job to meddle with fate, was it?

Wanda Sue eventually emerged from the bedroom. She'd showered, dressed and ate breakfast, ignoring the pancakes for Greek yogurt and an English muffin. She had slept poorly and was still feeling pangs of anger and anxiety, the corrosive residue from her heated confrontation with Max. It had occurred to her during the night that maybe she was being too hard on him. Now that she knew he had enough money to support them in the style she expected, she might want to hang around for a few more years, unless, of course, Tom was willing to divorce his wife right away.

In the clear light of day, however, she couldn't imagine staying with Max Gribbins for any longer than it took her attorney to dissolve this charade of a marriage. Finding the secret investment account was the key she needed to live life on her own terms. After the divorce, she'd end up with the house—which she'd probably sell—and at least half of everything else. Even if Tom Whitlow continued playing his waiting game, she'd be taken care of.

The raucous notes from Max's guitar could be heard outside on the lanai, and Wanda Sue figured he was trying to cope with the stress of what he knew was coming. Max had never been one to handle pressure very well. He usually erupted in fits of temper or stuck his head in the sand waiting for someone else to deal with the problem. This time he would have to face the world on her terms, so he might as well play that damn guitar while he could. If she had her way it would belong to her after the divorce.

Wanda Sue finished breakfast and did the one thing she'd planned on doing for a long, long time. She called her attorney and made an appointment to finalize the divorce proceedings. She made a mental note to leave the house early tomorrow morning since traffic on the Buckman was always crazy and she didn't want to be late for her 9:00 a.m. appointment.

CHAPTER NINE
The Buckman Bridge

It wasn't until Max was ready for bed—still occupying the guest bedroom—that he realized there had been no other news reports that day. This was uncommon since most days Walter took only a few breaks between reports. Of course most of them were of little consequence to him, not like the morning's big announcement. He didn't worry about it, deciding Walter deserved some time off.

He looked at the clock on the bedside table, calculating the hours until his wife's 8:30 demise. Poor Wanda Sue, but he was at peace with his decision. Lying in the dark, he rehearsed the lines he'd recite in his role of grief-stricken husband.

"You're all dressed up. Got a hot date?" Max asked.

Wanda Sue cast a withering glance in his direction. "It's none of your business, but I have an appointment in Jacksonville."

"This is awfully early for you. Must be something important."

"As I said, it's none of your business." She opened her purse and fished around for her keys.

Max approached her thinking this would be the last time he'd see Wanda Sue alive. He didn't know if he should say something special, something memorable like, *The Eagle has landed.* Or, *Here's looking at you, kid.* Or maybe, *Frankly, my dear, I don't give a damn.*

In the end he decided to play it straight and offer his soon-to-be ex-wife an apology.

"Listen, Wanda Sue." He touched her arm, but she pulled away. "I'm sorry about keeping that account from you. I know it was stupid. I don't want you to drive off this morning thinking I'm a complete asshole."

"Close enough, Max. Close enough." She turned and walked through the connecting door to the garage where her green Scion was parked.

Max watched her disappear into the garage thinking why did he even try to be nice to the bitch. He returned to the kitchen, switching on the small, but expensive Bose radio Wanda Sue kept on the counter next to the toaster oven. He fiddled with the dial until he found Jacksonville's all news station. He noted the time—8:05 a.m. Only 25 minutes before Wanda Sue took a nosedive into the river. He poured himself another cup of coffee and considered what he should wear to the funeral.

At 8:30 Max turned up the volume on the radio, edging closer to await the news. Fifteen minutes passed. Not a word of any accident on the Buckman Bridge. Max left the radio on, but hurried to the den where he turned the flat screen TV to Jacksonville's independent station. The former network affiliate had a habit of interrupting programming throughout the day and night for what it considered "Breaking News," which covered everything from an increase in gasoline prices to the results of the mayor's colonoscopy. A mobile unit would be dispatched at a moment's notice to cover school fights, traffic jams and wildfires. Surely, they would be on the scene to report on a sensational accident like this one.

Max kept listening and watching. 9:00 a.m. 9:15 a.m. Nothing.

Maybe he had the time wrong, he thought, but the 8:30 accident was imprinted on his brain, and trusty Walter Cronkite didn't make mistakes. Every single one of the reports on Max's personal news channel had been accurate to the minute, so why should he doubt this one? Perhaps, he figured, the gridlock on the bridge was so bad no news gatherers could get near the accident scene. But that didn't explain why the accident hadn't been reported and motorists warned to find an alternate route.

Max paced from the kitchen to the den, to his office and back to the kitchen, wishing he'd never given up smoking. The tension building inside him felt like a clogged pipe about to explode, building to the breaking point before spewing its contents everywhere. When he found himself chewing his nails, he knew he had to do something.

He went right to the source of his anxiety and called Wanda Sue's cell phone. The phone rang five times before her voice mail kicked in with the first few bars of The Kingslayers number one hit, "Never Give Up." Flustered, he clicked off without leaving a message. Max chewed on his lower lip for a moment wondering if the fact she didn't answer her phone was a sign she was dead, but decided she probably wouldn't have answered it anyway when his name popped up.

He dropped into a chair, his shoulders and head slumped forward in a posture of defeat. He pressed the heels of his hands to either side of his head, squeezing his skull as hard as he could as if trying to force the voice to provide an answer to his dilemma. His right leg began jerking up and down spasmodically, ruled by the twin rhythms of frustration and panic.

You can't sit here all day worrying yourself sick. Do something!

Max pushed himself out of the chair, fetched the keys to his black Hummer H2 and raced out to the garage. He cranked up the engine, hit the garage door opener and backed into the street, leaving a trail of rubber as he rocketed away from the house.

Twenty minutes and a dozen second guesses later, Max slipped into the I-295 southbound ramp for Jacksonville, the Buckman Bridge only minutes away. The steel-beam bridge was over 3 miles long and carried 125,000 cars a day on the east-west passage. Even without his aquaphobia, he avoided bridge whenever possible. You could count on traffic backing up at the exits at any hour of the day, but it was always worse during morning and evening rush hours. Gridlocks escalated tempers, fueling self-destructive behavior, multiplying road rage and contributing to frequent crashes. He remembered at least three deaths in the past two years.

Max glanced at the digital clock on his dashboard. It was nearly two hours past the time Wanda Sue was supposed to have drowned. Ahead of him, he saw no sign of any accident and the traffic, although heavy as usual, was moving at a steady pace.

On the bridge now, Max fought the urge to close his eyes, feeling the familiar waves of dread grip him by the throat. Water surrounded him. To his left and right, between the two ribbons of highway unfurling ahead of him into the horizon, he not only saw but also felt the steel blue water of the St. Johns River pulling at him.

He tried to purge the gruesome vision of the dead girl's face from his brain. *Nothing there. Only a bad dream*, he repeated, willing his eyes to stay focused on the road ahead. The morning sun made that difficult, dazzling him with reflected rays bursting through his tinted windshield directly into his eyes. Max lowered the visor, chancing a glance through the passenger side window at the four lanes of traffic traveling in the opposite direction. The westbound lanes moved smoothly with far fewer vehicles.

Despite the rush of frosty air from the Hummer's air conditioning unit, Max felt beads of sweat on his forehead and an uncomfortable dampness under his arms. He had lived in Northeast Florida for most of his life and knew the weather was a capricious and fickle thing. Last week the temperature had hovered in the mid 70s, but today his dash display indicated it was a scorching 92 degrees outside.

Despite the outside heat, he felt the shell of the Hummer closing in on him and rolled down his window. Hot air hit him in the face and he heard the sound of his own engine mixed with the clatter of wheels on the bridge. Max breathed deeply, fighting the feeling of claustrophobia blanketing him.

He drove on, eyes focused on the roadway, his resolve growing stronger as the dreaded feelings of aquaphobia subsided. In the distance he could see Jacksonville's skyline on the opposite bank. But there was still no sign of an accident, and the voice in his head—that once infallible voice—had remained silent since yesterday's pronouncement that Wanda Sue Gribbins had become another notch on the Buckman Bridge's railing.

It looked now like he could no longer trust Walter's prognostications. At this point, Max couldn't be sure the voice would ever return since it had never gone this long without a broadcast.

Just as this thought flitted through his mind, the familiar thrum of static buzzed through his head. "Damn!" Max blurted out. "Just as I was losing faith in you, old boy, here you come again. I hope it's good news this time."

The burst of static grew louder, more piercing than ever before. Max shook his head from side to side, trying to break the neurological circuit causing the unbearable noise. As his head shifted right toward the westbound traffic lanes, Max thought he saw a small boxy-looking vehicle out of the corner of his eye. The car zipped away from him. It was the same shade of green, and although he couldn't see the driver, he knew as well as he knew his name was Mad Max Gribbins that the car was a Scion and the driver was his very much alive wife.

He craned his neck around following the vehicle until Walter's voice suddenly burst through the racket in his head.

"Police are reporting that the driver of a Total Waste Solutions garbage truck apparently suffered a medical event while driving across Jacksonville's Buckman Bridge today."

Max heard the words, but they failed to totally register on him while he watched the green Scion driving away. With the words *Buckman Bridge* though, he turned his attention fully to the incoming news report.

"The thirty-two ton vehicle careened out of control, barreling across two lanes of traffic, pushing vehicles aside before plowing into …"

Garbage truck? The last report said a Ford Expedition plowed into Wanda Sue's car, flinging the little Scion over the railing. Now it was a garbage truck. He could only imagine what a monstrous garbage truck would do to the tiny vehicle.

"… a large black SUV that witnesses identified as a Hummer H2. The force of the crash flipped the SUV over twice where it …"

Moments before the voice completed the sentence Max saw a mammoth green shape hurtling toward him. Sixty-four thousand pounds of runaway garbage truck smashed into the Hummer. Max flew against the door, his head bouncing off the window. The air bag deployed with a great whoosh and puffs of acrid smoke filled the interior of the Hummer.

Max felt the Hummer swerve, the rear end fishtailing. The sheer weight and momentum of the garbage truck propelled the SUV in a 190-degree arc where it collided with two other cars. Max felt the sensation of centrifugal force as the car spun around. He heard the crunch of metal on metal, feeling his tank of a vehicle shudder with each collision. A fleeting thought swept through him that this was the reason he wanted a big heavy car. The Hummer weighed more than six thousand pounds, but that was no match against a 32-ton garbage truck.

He felt the H2 roll onto its side. His body somersaulted inside the SUV, his head slamming against the car's roof. He heard sheet metal ripping and plummeted to one side as the Hummer continued rolling, gaining speed as it flipped over a Ford Fusion and ricocheted into the fourth lane closest to the river.

Inside the Hummer, Max could only wait for the car to stop rolling. His head felt like it would explode and he forced a hand up to touch his temple where he'd collided with the window. His fingers came away covered with blood.

Max hurt all over. He thought he may have fractured a wrist and some ribs, and his right leg was twisted away from him at an unnatural angle. But he was still alive, and even though the Hummer continued rolling he knew the safety barrier would bring an end to this nightmare.

Max was right that the nightmare was nearing its end, but not quite as soon as he had hoped. The careening Hummer plowed into a GMC Sierra 1500, somersaulting over the long bed with such force the H2 flew into the air landing on its roof atop the guardrail.

The Buckman's rails are built to Federal safety standards of two feet eight inches and designed to bounce swerving vehicles back to the roadway in case of an accident. But the barriers were not built to stop flying vehicles.

Max felt the breath hammered out of him in the final collision. He had a sense of weightlessness for a moment as he hung between the roof of the SUV and the driver's seat. By some strange accident of physics, the H2 teetered on the top rail of the barrier. Suspended with one half of the oversized vehicle hanging over the roadway and the other half over the water, it balanced precariously for a long moment.

Through the cracked windshield Max saw the wide expanse of water stretching before him. He heard himself scream. Max couldn't remember the last time he prayed, but now he prayed with ardent fervor.

"Please God; don't let it fall into the water. Please! Please! Please!

Tears flowed from his eyes, mixing with the stream of blood gushing from the gash in his head.

The Hummer swayed toward the roadway as if in response to his prayers. He threw himself in the same direction feeling the vehicle shifting and gravity pulling it back onto the roadway.

Oh, thank …

He felt a sickening crunch. In the millisecond before the SUV toppled off the railing and began it's dive into the St. Johns River, Max glimpsed the words Total Waste Solutions on the side of the out of control garbage truck.

The Hummer flipped over once before plunging headlong into the dark water. This couldn't be happening to him, he thought. It was supposed to be Wanda Sue who died. That's what his prognosticating voice had told him.

The SUV hit the water with a thunderous crash and disappeared below the surface before bobbing up like a cork. Max knew his odds of survival were little to none if he was trapped inside the vehicle. The sheer weight of the Hummer would take him down to the bottom of the river some forty feet below. Fortunately his window was still down, but the seat belt held him tight across the waist and chest.

Water poured into the car through the open window and cracked floorboards.

"Help me," Max bellowed, though he knew he was beyond help.

He stabbed blindly at the seat belt release button, but nothing happened and he feared it had been damaged in the crash. The Hummer slipped below the surface once again. The entire compartment filled with black water.

Max held his breath while he banged at the release button over and over. He pulled desperately on the belt, slipping one shoulder out of the restraining seat belt, but he was still held fast at the waist. Lungs bursting, he made one more attempt to release the belt. His thumb pressed down and he heard a click. The seat belt released and Max floated up until his head banged against the roof lining where he found a pocket of air.

Greedily, Max inhaled as much air as his lungs would hold before pushing himself out the open window of the Hummer into the embrace of the St. Johns River, a place he'd hoped he'd never come near again. Fiery bolts of pain shot up his right leg. Stabbing lancets attacked his chest.

Max opened his eyes in the dark water trying to orient himself, fighting the rising panic that threatened to paralyze him. He saw the Hummer continue its descent to the floor of the river and kicked with his one good leg in the opposite direction. Above him was light and salvation.

He stroked madly through the water. He had no idea how deep he was, but he felt his air supply dwindling. Fighting the urge to open his mouth and breathe, Max pressed upwards, beating his arms, ignoring the pain and hoping for rescuers to find him.

But there were no rescuers. Nothing around him but the hateful water. His chest ached and he realized that whatever air was still in his lungs might be the last he'd ever breathe.

Almost there. Don't give up.

The light above him grew brighter and the tiny spark of hope he'd kept alive burst into flame. Only feet from the surface, Max stretched out his arms, hoping there would be rescuers waiting to help him out of the water. He was so close now he thought he saw the faces of people leaning over the railing.

A surge of relief poured over him and without realizing it he breathed through his nose. Immediately water rushed through his nostrils and down his esophagus. Max felt the cold water sloshing in his lungs and made another desperate lunge to the surface.

Something clenched the ankle of his damaged leg and pulled. Excruciating pain exploded through the leg. Max gasped and more water seeped into his mouth. He had no idea what had seized his leg, but it wouldn't let go. Could he have been entangled in floating debris? A shark? An alligator?

The grip on his ankle tightened even more and he felt himself pulled down into the dark waters. He closed his eyes and let himself drift away, knowing he was about to take his final breath.

Something touched Max's cheek. He opened his eyes and saw a hand with long fingers. The nails were painted black. A face appeared—the face of a young girl with long blonde hair, a broken nose and vacant blue eyes. The face of the girl in his nightmare.

Although her mouth didn't move, Max heard the dreaded phrase ring through his head as clear as old Walter's voice.

Help me … can't swim … don't leave me here to die

In his last moment of clarity, all the repressed details of his near-death experience came flashing back to him. He saw himself parking the red Corvette under the old oak trees by the river. He saw the girl emerge from the car, laughing at his drunken state. Max stumbled toward the girl.

He remembered wrapping his arms around her, forcing her across the hood of the sports car. Max could see her struggling to get away, her fists beating against his back as he pressed himself against her. He ignored her protests, reaching under her skirt. He grunted and swore when she bit deep into his shoulder. He pulled away and the girl broke and ran toward the water.

Max remembered rushing after her and catching her as the river lapped at their feet. Furious and too stoned to care, he grabbed her by the hair, pulling her farther into the river until the water was up to his neck. The girl with the blonde hair fought him, scratching at his face. He felt her nails scrape a groove down one cheek before he pushed her head under water.

She came up gasping for air, screaming at him.

"Don't. Can't swim."

She clawed at him again, this time leaving a bloody streak on his neck. Seething with rage, Max swung wildly at her head, feeling the crunch of bone and cartilage give way. Bubbles of blood oozed from her nose and he pushed her under again, holding her there until she stopped struggling.

Max could see the entire scene flash before him in that last second before he was forced to open his mouth. He remembered the moon was bright and there was a decrepit old pier with three posts where fishing rods leaned. As he clambered onto dry land, he heard her crying far behind him.

Help me ... can't swim ... don't leave me here to die

He thought he heard the guitars of the three mariachis as he took a breath and water filled his lungs.

CHAPTER TEN
Epilogue

Max's memorial service was a surprisingly upbeat affair. All of the members of The Kingslayers arrived in a white limousine the size of a city block. One by one they rose to regale the mourners with hilarious stories of their former lead guitarist, many of them involving Max under the influence of one mind altering substance or another. To the delight of everyone, they ended the service with an unplugged version of "Never Give Up." Wanda Sue dabbed at the tears that welled up in her eyes. Her neighbor, Tom Whitlow, sitting behind her, put a hand on her shoulder to comfort her.

Two weeks later, Wanda Sue had packed up most of Max's clothes and other belongings she didn't want and carted them off to Good Will. She decided his guitars and the Grammy he shared for Album of the Year were valuable and thought she might sell them on eBay or Craig's List. She looked back on those early days with more than a little fondness and nostalgia, but now she was prepared for the next chapter in her life.

Wanda Sue had already met with the insurance company's representative, who assured her the death benefits would be arriving soon. Early in their marriage, when Max still played with the band, she had talked him into buying a million-dollar insurance policy. She convinced him that all the big rock stars carried that much insurance and so should he.

She'd quickly tracked down his broker at Smith Barney who told her about Max's lucky investments with the pharmaceutical company and the gold stocks. Then there was the mysterious $200,000 in cash he'd deposited in the account only days before his accident. Almost overnight, Wanda Sue had been transformed from stressed-out housewife battling a tightfisted husband to a widowed millionaire. She liked the feeling.

What she didn't like was the lethargy that had settled in unexpectedly, dragging her down, leaving her feeling confused and uncertain. The change in her personal life should have left her electric with giddiness. Instead she moped around the house, nursing what doctors were calling incipient migraine symptoms, and drinking more to counter her depressions.

Her affair with Tom Whitlow had been put on hold since Max's death. Despite his almost daily calls, Wanda Sue thought it was wise to let him stew for a while. She understood clearly what he wanted, and to be honest, she missed their passionate lovemaking nearly as much as he did. But until her next-door neighbor decided to move their relationship above the horizontal level and divorce his wife, she wasn't going to give him the satisfaction of bedding her.

On this day, nearly a month after they'd buried Max, Wanda Sue sat alone on her lanai watching the sun disappear behind a mantle of vermillion clouds. She took another sip from her glass of chardonnay—her third glass, or was it her fourth? As usual, her thoughts returned to Tom Whitlow. Should she continue to pursue him as a potential husband? Or should she move on with her life, possibly sell the house and relocate? Do some traveling, perhaps. She'd always wanted to see Venice and Paris.

Her options were totally open, but she liked Tom and didn't want to give up on him. He was funny and sweet in a way Max had never been. She believed they could make it work if Tom could just wriggle out from under his marriage.

She tilted the glass back and finished the wine in one long gulp. She felt a little tipsy, but she needed the liquid courage to prepare her for tonight's rendezvous with Tom. She'd been feeling a bit under the weather when he called that morning. He told her he was driving Dana to the airport for a 6:30 flight to Dallas, and wanted to see her when he returned.

"We need to talk," is what he said. "And I think you'll like what I'm going to say."

She tried to wheedle it out of him, but Tom only laughed and told her to be patient, that he'd knock on her door when he returned.

Tom's tone buoyed her spirits. He's finally going to divorce his wife, she told herself. Wanda Sue didn't expect Dana would fight the divorce since it had been a long distance marriage for years. She suspected Dana had her own lover—or lovers—to keep her company when she was on the road.

The thought of Tom's visit filled her with anticipation, especially since Tom's idea of a conversation always revolved around pillow talk. It had been a long time and she ached to be with him again.

As soon as Tom entered the house they were in each other's arms. He nearly tore her blouse in his eagerness to get her clothes off. She managed to pull him into the bedroom where their lovemaking was as intense as the first time they'd done it on the floor in his ham radio room.

Sweating and out of breath, Tom rolled off of her, but she pulled him back, unable to let him go.

"My god, Wanda, you were like a mad woman there. If we went at it any harder, we'd have caught fire."

"I thought I smelled smoke," she said.

They lay snuggled together until their heartbeats slowed to a more normal rate. The wine and the lovemaking had helped, but Wanda Sue still felt out of sorts.

Tom raised himself off the bed on his elbows and looked into her face. "I've decided," he said.

"Oh, what have you decided?"

A little smile played across Tom's face, and Wanda Sue thought he looked like a little boy in the dim bedroom light. Tom was speaking again, but in her mind's eye Max's face suddenly appeared and she heard the wailing of his guitar solo in "Never Give Up."

Where did that come from?

"Did you hear me? I said I'm going to ask Dana for a divorce when she comes home from her business trip."

Wanda Sue sat up, the sheet falling away from her naked body. "I'm sorry, what were you saying?"

Tom was staring at her in the strangest way.

"What the hell's wrong with you, Wanda Sue? For the past year you've begged me to divorce my wife and when I tell you that I will, you're not even listening."

"I'm sorry, Tom. I'm just not myself these days. I'm having trouble concentrating, and …"

"And what?"

"I don't know. I'm probably just coming down with something."

Tom shook his head, leaned over and kissed her lightly on the lips. "Listen, baby. Even though you didn't love Max, I'm sure his death came as a shock. That would screw up anybody's mind."

"Maybe, but I've been hearing this strange humming in my ears. Do you think I'm getting Max's tinnitus? It's not contagious, is it?"

"Tinnitus? I doubt that." Tom laughed and gave her ear a playful tug. "Your ears are too cute to be bothered by the nasty tinnitus bug."

She grasped his hand and held it tightly. Wanda Sue matched his laugh with one of her own. "I know you're going to say this is crazy, but sometimes the humming sounds like someone whispering."

They both laughed again at the absurdity of the notion. Tom blew into her ear and rolled back on top of her.

About the Author

Parker Francis is the author of the Quint Mitchell Mystery series. The first in the series, the award-winning MATANZAS BAY, is set in the nation's oldest city of St. Augustine, Florida and reached #3 on Amazon's Top 100 list in the Hard-Boiled Mystery category. BRING DOWN THE FURIES, the second in the series, was released in 2012, as was the Quint Mitchell novella, BLUE CRABS AT MIDNIGHT. Parker followed that with the third Quint Mitchell thriller, HURRICANE ISLAND, which was called "the perfect storm of a mystery."

In a prior life, Parker enjoyed a career in broadcasting working as a public affairs and documentary producer, reporter, fundraiser, and producer of an acclaimed jazz festival. Under his own name (Victor DiGenti) he wrote three adventure/fantasies with a feline protagonist. His novels — *Windrusher, Windrusher and the Cave of Tho-hoth,* and *Windrusher and the Trail of Fire* have won multiple awards and attracted readers of all ages.

Keep reading for a preview of *Hurricane Island.*

An Excerpt from *Hurricane Island*

One

Cedar Key, Florida

Saturday, September 22, 7:10 a.m.

THE ROAR OF THE twin Yamahas shattered the early morning stillness. Three brown pelicans chirped angrily and launched themselves from the far end of the marina with ungainly strokes, circling overhead for a moment before winging across the choppy waters of the bay.

A skilled detective learns to pay attention to his gut. As the *Island Hopper* rose and fell against the dock, my gut was raising warning flags. I should have paid attention.

We were standing on the dock of the Cedar Key Marina, a tiny fishing village billing itself as the island community where time stands still. Woody Carpenter gunned the engines again. He grinned his crooked schoolboy smile at me, looking like a casting director chose him for the part of a fishing boat captain—mirrored sunglasses, a salt-and-pepper beard covering his tanned face and a battered Atlanta Braves ball cap on his head. He waved me aboard.

"Time's a-wasting, Quint. The fish have been up for hours."

I watched Woody's wife pull out of the parking lot, the sun glinting off the roof of the Lexus SUV. My on-again-off-again girlfriend, Serena, sat on the passenger side while Kate and Woody's daughter, Delia, was strapped into a car seat in the back. No seasickness for them, I thought, before turning and scrambling aboard Woody's 28-foot Parker Pilot.

We were soon under way, chugging by the stilted restaurants nestled along Dock Street.

"There she is," Woody said, pointing to the blue-roofed Laughing Gull Café. He squeezed off an ear-splitting blast on the air horn and goosed the engines.

When Serena and I arrived on the island yesterday, the Carpenters took us to The Gull—as the locals call it—for dinner, and Kate gave us a quick history lesson on the restaurant she and Woody owned. Kate's father had operated the restaurant for years before his stroke. Then Kate and her twin brothers, Donnie and Dougie—yeah, that's their names—took over, with Kate doing most of the heavy lifting.

She said the restaurant was sliding into Chapter 11 before she married Woody. Technically, Woody now owned The Laughing Gull Café, but he'd made it clear he didn't want anything to do with running a restaurant.

Woody spoke up above the roar of the engines. "Gotta tell you, Quint, I'm glad you took me up on my offer. It's been a long time."

"I'm glad you called," I said.

"And when you asked if you could bring your girlfriend along, I had no idea you were dating Beyoncé."

I laughed. "She's a doll, isn't she?"

"So how long have you two been an item?"

"This is the second time around for us, and we're taking it slow. See what develops."

He nodded, though I could tell he wasn't sure what to make of the two of us together. "You seem really happy," I said, changing the subject.

"Yeah, best thing that happened to me, moving down here from Atlanta. After Anne died I struggled to stay afloat, treading water until ..." He turned away from me. Bright shards of sun scudded across the water, reflecting off his shades.

"That's when I decided to start over. Leave Atlanta and all its bad memories behind."

A drug dealer who was too dedicated to his own product murdered Anne.

That was seven years ago, when Woody was still a detective with the Atlanta Police Department. He's never given me all the details, but I learned from a friend in the Georgia Bureau of Investigation, otherwise known as the GBI, that Woody tracked down his wife's murderer and killed him in a shootout. There was collateral damage, according to my source, and instead of fighting a suspension he turned in his badge and gun, then quit the force.

"And look at you now—charter boat captain, restaurant mogul, and father."

He smiled broadly. "One lucky sonnavabitch, aren't I?"

We sipped coffee from our travel mugs, Woody sitting in the cushioned ladder-back helm seat, one hand resting on the wheel. I stood next to him, holding on to the back of his seat to keep my balance as the boat humped over the waves.

"Serena and Kate seemed to have hit it off," I said. "I'm glad they'll have a chance to get to know one another better."

After dropping Delia at prekindergarten, the two women were connecting with Ruth Foley, Kate's friend and business partner, before driving to Gainesville for the day.

Woody nodded. "The only drawback is Ruth Foley tagging along."

"Sounds like you and Ruth aren't exactly bosom buddies."

"She rubs me the wrong way. One of those bleeding-heart liberal types with a big mouth. I'm sure she'll slobber all over Serena."

He glanced at me, and I understood the not-so-veiled reference to Serena's mixed-race ethnicity. I didn't say anything and we continued bumping over the water in silence for a few minutes.

When he spoke again, Woody played the part of the friendly tour guide, steering the boat past a series of islands, calling out their names. The cabin door was open, and I stood close with my coffee, straining to hear him above the sound of the wind and the two Yamaha outboards.

He pointed to one of the larger islands. "There used to be a thriving community there. Lumber mills were big then—lots of cedar, as you'd expect. A pencil company in New Jersey built a mill on the island to supply wood for the factory. Now it's mostly infested by bugs and birds."

"Huh."

He jutted his chin toward the open waters dotted with small islands. "During the Seminole Indian Wars, the Army built a detention center for the captured Indians on Seahorse Key. Today it's a bird sanctuary and marine research center."

He steered the boat past one of the larger islands. Dozens of birds rose from the trees, flying toward open waters before circling back to the island.

"The old-timers tell a story about a Seminole war chief named Alligator, whose family was wiped out by the Army. He retaliated with a series of raids, slashing his way through the region. You might call him an equal opportunity paleface exterminator, killing men and women alike. They said he'd mark his kills by leaving an alligator tooth next to the bodies."

"Sounds like a local legend," I said.

"I'm sure it is, but it was a bloody time in the region's history with atrocities on both sides, I'm sure. The war went on for years, until attrition set in and the hurricane came along."

"Hurricane?"

"A bastard of a hurricane hit the area in 1842. Wiped out the Army's outpost and most of the town."

Woody steered us past another island, gunning the engines as we moved into open waters. The cabin protected us from the wind and spray jetting along both sides of the boat.

"Hurricanes seem to have a natural affinity for this part of the state," Woody shouted at me, his voice rising over the roar of the engines. "Cedar Key's been nearly wiped out by some nasty storms over the last two hundred years, but the town keeps coming back stronger than ever."

"And now there's another hurricane in the Gulf? Talk about good timing for my visit."

"Not to worry. I checked the latest reports this morning, and the storm hasn't moved in hours. The meteorologists say there's a good chance it'll turn toward Texas."

Woody pulled back on the throttle as we passed a line of PVC pipes sticking out of the water. Each one had an identical bright orange sign attached to it.

"What's that?"

"Clam beds. Aquaculture is big business around here. Clam farmers grow the little boogers from larvae to adults. When they get to a certain size they're put in bags and secured to the bottom of the bay with PVC pipes until they mature."

"Who knew?"

"Your ignorance of Cedar Key knows no bounds, my friend." Woody's mouth twitched in a smile, and I imagined his blue eyes twinkling behind the sunglasses.

"How about some more coffee?" He reached for my cup.

"I'm good."

"Then take the wheel. I have to use the head."

The marine radio squawked before he'd stepped away, and he settled back into the helm seat as a voice boomed out of the built-in speaker.

"Come in, *Island Hopper*, this is Chief Parsons. Are you there, Woody?"

Woody reached across the console for the microphone and keyed the button to talk. "This is Woody. Go ahead, Joe."

"What's your twenty?"

Woody scanned the water as though looking for a directional sign. "About a mile past North Key, bearing northwest. What's going on, Joe?"

"I need you to turn around and head back to town. Pronto."

"Can't it wait? We're on our way to do some fishing. Should be back by three."

"Listen to me, Woody. Turn your damn boat around. This isn't a request."

"You're the chief," Woody said, "but can you tell me what's going on?"

A low hum sputtered from the speaker while we waited for the chief's reply. Another boat passed us going in the opposite direction and honked twice. I watched the water boiling in the boat's wake, the *Island Hopper* jouncing over its waves.

The radio crackled to life and Chief Parsons' voice replaced the static. "I'll explain when you get here, but there's been an …"

Parsons' voice slipped away, static hissing and popping through the speaker. I thought we might have lost him, when we heard his voice break through again.

"There's been an incident at your house."